"Take the theological forcefulness of Bonh
with the imaginative whimsy of C. S. Lewis
Spurgeon, and you get Matt Mikalatos. He is a gifted writer, a true Christian, with a first-rate mind. *Imaginary Jesus* is a startlingly original, comedic, and theologically true tour de force. It marks the debut of one of today's most prominent young Christian writers."

Gary Thomas—author of *Sacred Marriage* and *Pure Pleasure*

"If there is such a thing as a holy romp, this is it. I laughed, I applauded and cheered, I thanked God. Every Christian I know will want to read this one!"

Phyllis Tickle—author of *The Great Emergence*

"Matt Mikalatos writes like a happy-go-lucky C. S. Lewis. *Imaginary Jesus* is relentlessly funny, with surprisingly profound spiritual insights."

Josh D. McDowell—author and speaker

"Matt Mikalatos has written a funny, surprising, gutsy tale. Through his writing, I recognized many of my own false assumptions and shallow beliefs, and possibly even more importantly, I really enjoyed the journey."

Shauna Niequist—author of *Cold Tangerines*

"I didn't know what I was getting into when I started reading *Imaginary Jesus* by Matt Mikalatos. By the second page, I was hooked by its humor and challenging insights. Be prepared to have your relationship with Jesus enriched and enlarged by this fun and fascinating look at how we tend to picture Jesus on our own terms."

Tremper Longman—Robert H. Gundry Professor of Biblical Studies, Westmont College

"*Imaginary Jesus* not only entertained me to the point that I was embarrassed by my public outbursts of laughter, but it also challenged my faulty thinking on who Jesus was and is. Matt's zany sense of humor was only outdone by the fact that he made so much sense! I'm grateful he let us into his wacky universe!!"

Chris Zaugg—Campus Crusade for Christ; executive director of Keynote

"Warning: Reading this book can cause one to lose their false faith. In *Imaginary Jesus*, Matt Mikalatos confronts the images of Jesus he created over the years in order to reveal the radical rebel who came to redeem the world."

Becky Garrison—author of *Jesus Died For This?: A Satirist's Search for the Risen Christ*

"Wise and profound—and I don't say that lightly. Creative in its use of the surreal, this imaginative tale is also that rare thing: a glimpse at what the process of maturing in Christian faith looks like. Matt Mikalatos' book will hold up long after the imaginary Jesuses in current vogue have shuffled toward the history section."

Anna Broadway, author of *Sexless in the City*

"Crazy and creative and utterly captivating. *Imaginary Jesus* is an entertaining annihilation of all the false and frustrating idols that need to be kicked around a little more."

Dale Ahlquist—president of the American Chesterton Society

"Matt Mikalatos is a crazy man. But he is a wise crazy man. *Imaginary Jesus* is a crazy book. But don't let that fool you. It has a powerful message that is desperately needed for our insane times. So just go with it and let Matt take you on a hilariously serious journey through the oddly firing synapses of his brain. And don't be surprised if you lose some unnecessary baggage along the way."

Coleman Luck—Hollywood screenwriter; executive producer of *The Equalizer* and *Gabriel's Fire*; author of *Angel Fall*

"Matt Mikalatos has an incredible gift that is highlighted throughout *Imaginary Jesus*. While this book is hilarious, it will also cause you to stop dead in your tracks and evaluate what you really believe about Jesus."

Pete Wilson—pastor of Cross Point Community Church, Nashville, TN

"With uncompromising awareness and hilarious creativity, Mikalatos delivers a tour de force that is accessible, entertaining, and thought provoking. You'll laugh out loud at Mikalatos's brilliant humor, but watch out—while you're laughing, he'll hit you square in the jaw with a solid right hook when he presents you with your own mythology about Jesus."

Coach Culbertson—editor-in-chief, Coach's Midnight Diner; ccPublishing, NFP

"Perhaps the funniest Christian book of all time. Including the future. But more enjoyable if read in the present."

Keith Bubalo—national director of Worldwide Student Network

"Imaginative, thought-provoking, funny, and especially convicting. This book exposes my own imaginary Jesus, as well as the many others out there. It reads like an updated version of Phillips's *Your God Is Too Small*, only with a lot more wit and creativity. Matt helps all of us see our own propensity to idolatry, and brings us back to the real Jesus."

Dr. John E. Johnson—associate professor of pastoral theology at Western Seminary; lead pastor of Village Baptist Church

"*Imaginary Jesus* is the most powerful and clever book I've read this year. I am already recommending it to everyone I know. Which now includes you. Read it."

Lead singer of Page CXVI

"*Imaginary Jesus* is a fast, wild, unnerving ride. Think J. B. Phillips (*Your God Is Too Small*) on six shots of espresso running crazy through the streets of Portland, Oregon."

David Sanford—author of *If God Disappears: 9 Faith Wreckers and What to Do about Them*

"When I read *Imaginary Jesus*, I laughed so hard milk came out of my nose . . . and I wasn't even drinking any."

Adam Sabados—just some guy

A not-quite-true story . . .

Imaginary Jesus

Matt Mikalatos

MATT MIKALATOS

BARNA
AN IMPRINT OF TYNDALE HOUSE PUBLISHERS, INC.

To
Concordia
University.
Enjoy!

To Concordia University Enjoy

Visit Tyndale's exciting Web site at www.tyndale.com.

TYNDALE is a registered trademark of Tyndale House Publishers, Inc.

Barna and the Barna logo are trademarks of George Barna.

BarnaBooks is an imprint of Tyndale House Publishers, Inc.

Imaginary Jesus

Designed by Beth Sparkman

Published in association with the literary agencies of Wes Yoder of The Ambassador Literary Agency, 1107 Battlewood Street, Franklin, TN 37069 and Esther Fedorkevich, Fedd and Company Inc., 9759 Concord Pass, Brentwood, TN 37027.

Some names, characters, places, and incidents in this book are the product of the author's imagination. In fact, that's a major plot point of the book. Others are based on the author's memory of events and experiences, though he has changed these when it pleased him or the story demanded it. Sometimes it's hard to tell which is which. Hint: the talking donkey is made up.

Library of Congress Cataloging-in-Publication Data

Mikalatos, Matt.
Imaginary Jesus / Matt Mikalatos.
p. cm.
ISBN 978-1-4143-3563-6 (pbk.)
1. Jesus Christ—Fiction. 2. Imaginary companions—Fiction. 3. Portland (Or.)—Fiction. I. Title.
PS3613.I45I43 2010
813'.6—dc22 2009044448

Printed in the United States of America.

16 15 14 13 12 11 10

7 6 5 4 3 2 1

To the Hate Club—
the most bitter,
vicious, mean-spirited,
poorly tempered,
merciless friends
a guy could ever
hope to find.

Keep up the excellent work.

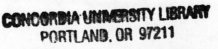

CHAPTER ZERO

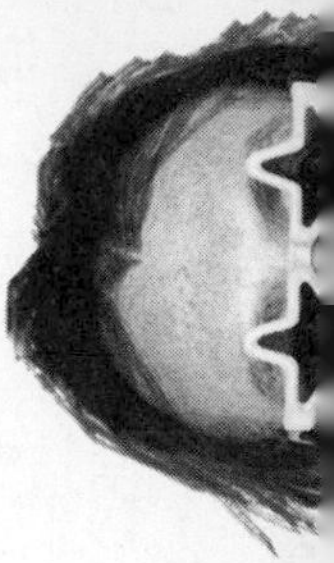

At the Red and Black

Jesus and I sometimes grab lunch at the Red and Black Café on Twelfth and Oak. It's decorated in revolutionary black and red, with posters and pictures of uprisings on the walls. The menu is vegan, which means that there are no animal products in the food. No meat, in other words. No honey, for that matter, because we don't want to steal from the hardworking bees.

The employees run the restaurant like a commune. There's no manager, and no one's in charge. I like to pick up the books and zines they sell and pretend to be a hard-core Portlander. Jesus likes the funky Portland vibe, and he thinks the socialist ethic that runs it is cute. He also likes the painting of Bruce Springsteen next to the counter, which has the caption, "The Only Boss We Listen To." He laughs at that every single time.

I was sitting by the round table with the chessboard painted on it, and Jesus was sitting across from me, his legs crossed and one sandaled foot bouncing to the music. I had my Bible open in front of me but sort of pushed behind a notebook so no one could see it. If someone figured out it wasn't a copy of Marx, I was pretty sure I might get stoned, and not from the secondhand smoke. Jesus had just put his earbuds in when the waitress brought me my vegan chili. This is the price you pay to be cool in this town. I took a bite, wished it had some meat in it, and poured as much Tapatío into it as I could stand. As I stirred the taste into my food, I realized that the worst possible thing had happened. They had forgotten my chips.

"They forgot my tortilla chips."

Jesus tossed his hair back and pulled an earbud out. "What was that?"

"They forgot my tortilla chips."

"I thought that might happen." He smiled.

"I'm going to ask them to bring some out."

Jesus smiled that same serene, knowing smile and shook his head. He does that sometimes. He doesn't overtly disagree with my actions, but I still get the feeling he's unhappy with me. Which annoys me. I took another bite of chili, and around my (meatless) mouthful I said, "What? What's wrong with asking for my tortilla chips?"

"Leave the poor communists alone," he said. "So they forgot your chips, so what? Show them how a nice Christian doesn't throw a fit when he's wronged."

"Humph." Under my breath I added, "Maybe you could turn my napkin into some tortilla chips."

"Then how would you wipe the chili off your chin?"

He was right. Chili was dripping off my chin. I wiped it off with my sleeve, just to teach him a lesson. He smiled and replaced his earbuds, and I turned my attention back to my Bible, which was weird with him sitting right across the table. It was like giving him a chance to talk when here I was, talking to him.

"You seem cranky today," Jesus said. "Are you angry with me?"

"You should know, Mr. Omniscience."

"I'd like you to tell me," he answered kindly.

"You know why I'm upset with you," I said darkly, not liking the turn this conversation had taken. I tried to find something to distract me, which is always easy at the good ol' Red and Black.

The best thing about the Red and Black is the customers. I worked at a comic book store back in the day, and I miss the steady stream of weirdos, misfits, and losers tromping through to talk about Dr. Doom. No one at the Red and Black wants to talk about Dr. Doom. That childish comic-book villain has been replaced by whomever happens to be president of the United States at any given moment. I sometimes hope that a future president will become fiercely disfigured and choose to wear a scowling metal mask to disguise his acid-scarred face. It would add a little melodrama to the Portland political scene.

The other best thing, if I could be allowed two best things, is that no one notices Jesus when we're at the restaurant together. He sits there with his iPod, smiling to himself, and no one notices the way he's dressed or the shiny glow of his halo getting all over everything.

A commotion at the counter broke my concentration. Commotion at the counter is part of life at the Red and Black, and to be honest, this is the third thing that is best: I often get distracted from my Bible and see something exciting. The most common source of commotion is the fact that the Red and Black refuses to take credit cards. To add to the insult, they will allow you to get money from your bank account by typing your ATM code into a pad connected to the cash register. After charging you a monstrous fee, they hand you cash out of the register. Why you can't use the same ATM pad to merely make a purchase is unclear. The downtown Suits who eat here get bent out of shape because the Red and Black doesn't participate in our financial system the way Big Business requires.

But the problem today came from a big-boned man, knotted with muscle, his black beard streaked with gray and spilling onto his wide chest. He wore dirty work jeans and a dark blue shirt that strained to contain him. "What do you mean 'no salmon'? This is the Pacific Northwest." He leaned in close to the woman taking his order, who gave him a look so weighted with disdain it could barely make it the seven inches from her eyes to his.

"We're vegan," she said. "*Vegan*. No meat. No animal products. *Fish* are *animals*."

The man looked like his eyes were going to bulge out of his head and slap her, but he took a deep breath and leaned back. "No fish. Okay. I'll get a glass of water and think about it." He walked to the side of the counter and poured himself a cup, then, to my chagrin, looked over and caught me staring. His eyes darted to my table, saw my Bible, and a wide grin broke out on his face. *Oh, great*. He was a Christian.

There aren't a lot of Christians in Portland, which means that when we see each other there's an obligatory minority dance that goes on. At the very least you have to raise your eyebrows and tip your chin up at one another. Some genres of Christian require that you talk about how hard life is in Portland (which it isn't). Some want to sit down and talk about their favorite book or the latest thing they learned on The KROS. That's our radio station. It's like a Christian ghetto on the airwaves. Safe for young people, positive words, okay music.

"Jesus," I hissed. "Keep that guy from coming over here."

Jesus looked over at the guy, who was only a few steps away now, and rolled his eyes. "Oh, man. Not him." He stood up. "Listen, I'm going to go check the parking meter."

I almost spilled my chili. "*What*? You can't leave me here with him."

Jesus looked at me sternly. "You prayed not to get a ticket while parked illegally in front of the café."

"I also prayed that there would be some quarters squirreled away in my car and *someone* didn't provide."

Jesus pointed his finger at me. "Watch it, Mikalatos. You know I don't care for your back talk." Then he stood up, and with a swirl of his robes he walked out the door, just as the hairy bear of a Christian man squeezed himself in at my table.

"Pete Jonason." He held out a powerful hand as wide as my plate. I shook it, doing my best to look incredibly busy. I could tell he worked the docks or something. A pungent smell of salt, fish, and ocean hung around him.

"Matt," I said.

He took a drink of his water, made a face, and spit it back into his cup. "They put some sort of chemicals in the drink."

He was right. The water had a weird taste. "I think it's rose water or something. They're completely organic here. I assume they wouldn't use chemicals."

Pete leaned back, his dark eyes staring at me with an unblinking ferocity that made me uncomfortable. I took another bite of chili. "You make a lot of assumptions, Matt."

He forgot about the water, took another sip, grunted, and spit it into his cup. He nodded in the direction of the door. Jesus stood out there, talking to a traffic cop who appeared to be writing a ticket for my truck. "I see that Jesus is wearing the traditional robes and powder blue sash today."

I choked on my chili. "You can *see* him?"

Pete cracked his enormous knuckles. "Sure. Just like anybody who's paying attention." He scratched behind his head with one big hand, the other resting lightly on the table. "Can I ask you a question?"

I sighed and closed my Bible. "Yeah."

"Why does your Jesus still wear a robe?"

"What do you mean?" I looked at Jesus, who had reentered the café. He flashed me a quick grin, which I took to mean he had taken care of the parking ticket, and sat down at a table across the café, by the window. Meaning I was stuck here with Pete the Christian.

"What I mean is, here's God, the creator of the universe. He becomes a human being and lives on Earth for thirty-three years. He completely assimilates to human culture. Wears our clothes. Wears a body like ours. Eats our food. But here he is, two thousand years later, and he's still wearing robes and a sash. Seems like he might put on a pair of jeans every once in a while. They're a great invention, jeans."

I watched Jesus thoughtfully. "That *is* weird. I guess I never thought about it."

Pete leaned in close, and I could smell the overpowering aroma on his breath when he said, "Let's go ask him about it."

I sighed. "Okay." We stood and walked over to him. Jesus smiled and offered me the chair across from him, and Pete towered over us, his arms crossed over his barrel chest. "This is Pete," I said.

"We've met." Jesus nodded.

"I don't recall," Pete said.

"We were just talking," I said, "and Pete asked me why you still wear two-thousand-year-old clothing. We were talking about the innovation of jeans, and we thought you might like them."

Jesus laughed. "It's just that these robes are so comfortable."

Pete looked outside. "Pretty rainy out there. You're wearing desert clothes. Aren't you cold?"

"Ha ha," Jesus said. "You need to read your Bible more, Pete. You may recall where it says, 'I, the Lord, do not change.'"

An excellent point, and straight out of the Bible. Score one for Jesus. I looked to Pete, who was scowling. "That verse doesn't refer to changing clothes," Pete said.

Jesus studied his fingernails, pretending to look for dirt. "Why don't you let me do the Scripture interpretation, Pete."

"Matt, let me ask you something," Pete said. "Is this guy better than you at anything?"

I thought carefully. "He's certainly nicer than me. And he has this way of expressing disapproval without actually saying anything. I've never been able to do that." I examined Jesus' face for a minute, his blue eyes shining merrily. "He has better hair. Mine is so fine and thin, and his is thick and silky."

"You're not the real Jesus." Pete grabbed a chair from another table and scooted in close, practically in Jesus' face. I put a hand on his arm and told him to calm down, but he ignored me and said, "What exactly do you want from my friend Matt here?"

Jesus stared at him. "I have plans to prosper him, plans for peace. I want him to be happy and rich. If he follows my instructions, that's exactly what will—"

Pete punched Jesus hard, in the face, causing his head to snap to the right and bounce off the window. I jumped up to intervene. Pete dragged Jesus from the table, and Jesus kicked over his chair, feet flailing. Pete had him in a bear hug, and Jesus elbowed him in the stomach. Pete lost his grip, grabbed Jesus by the hair, and slammed him to the ground. I shoved Pete with all my strength and he stumbled backward, flipping over a table and shattering a chair on the way down.

I helped Jesus up. "Are you okay? You should have called down some angels to protect you."

With a guttural roar, Pete launched himself across the table, straight for Jesus' head. Jesus sidestepped, turned, and ran out the door. Pete shook himself off and rose to go after him, but before he could leave, I picked up a leg from the broken chair and clocked him as hard as I could right in the back of the head. That didn't stop him, but it did slow him down enough for Jesus to get a good head start. I watched as he gathered his robes in his hands and ran like crazy, his white legs flashing out, his sandals eating the pavement like a dog licking ice cream.

Pete stood up, rubbing his head. He glared at me and then at the rapidly retreating Jesus. "Damn it," he said and kicked the table.

"You shouldn't curse."

"Sometimes a curse is called for. That—" Pete pointed out the window at the racing back of my Lord—"that was an imaginary Jesus, my friend. I choose my words carefully, and I said what I meant. And now that we're onto him, he's going to run."

I crossed my arms and frowned. "I've known Jesus for a long time. What makes you think that you know him better than I do?"

"Because," Pete said, headed for the door, "I'm the apostle Peter."

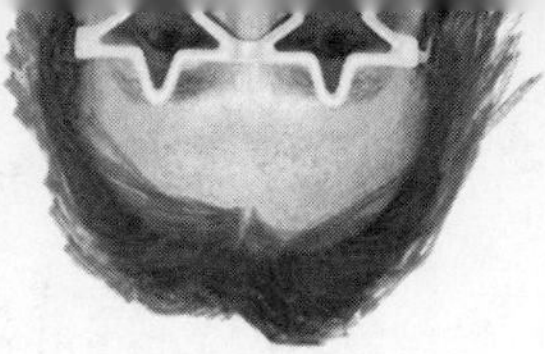

CHAPTER ONE

Following Jesus

I jumped in the truck and the so-called apostle slid in on the passenger side. I know I should have been stunned to have some wacko in my car who claimed to be from the first century, but there just wasn't time to think about it because Jesus was running north on Twelfth. It's a one-way street and I had parked facing the wrong way. It's a long story and it involved a great deal of fist shaking at various fellow Portlanders. Suffice it to say, I had slammed the truck into gear and was now headed west on Stark.

"Not that way!" Pete yelled. "He's headed north!"

"I know, but I'll head him off by going up Eleventh." Eleventh is a one-way street, too, headed south. I forgot about that. So I sped through the intersection and turned north on Tenth. I punched the gas and nearly ran over a cyclist. The streets of Portland are narrow, and the cyclist only survived by running into a parked car and flying up and over it onto the sidewalk.

"Where is he going?"

"You're the one who's been following him for two thousand years, you tell me."

"I've been following the *real* Jesus," Pete said. "I have no idea what your imaginary one will do."

We passed Ankeny Street, and Pete yelled out, "There he is, still headed north!"

"There's no way. No human being can run that fast." Then I thought about what I was saying, and I slowed the car down. "No *human being*. Pete, are you sure that's not the real Jesus?"

Pete hit the dashboard in frustration. "Would the real Jesus run away from a fight?"

I pulled the car over. I needed to think. "I guess he would turn the other cheek." *But wait.* "Maybe he would have a sword that comes out of his mouth and smites people."

Pete groaned. "Do you remember that part in the Bible where it says, 'Jesus girded his loins and ran'?"

"No."

"Can you think of any moment in which Jesus ran?"

"Hmm. You know in the Prodigal Son story, where the father runs to his see his son?"

Pete snorted. "Is Jesus running *toward* you right now?"

"No."

"That ain't Jesus. And if you want to hang out with the real thing, we need to deal with that faker."

I thought about this. I loved Jesus. Not the fake one. At least, I didn't think it was the fake one I was in love with. And if I had been hanging out with some imposter, I wanted to catch him and make him pay. I looked down at the dash. A thin pink piece of paper sat under my windshield wiper. A parking ticket. I jumped out of the car and snatched it. Fifty bucks. I lifted it toward the sky and waved it in a clenched fist. "IMAGINARY JESUS! He can't even fix my parking tickets!"

I leaped into the cab and tires squealed as I turned onto Burnside. Jesus looked back and his eyes widened in terror. He could see the angry burn in my eyes and the parking ticket clenched against the steering wheel. Jesus ran up alongside a cyclist, grabbed him by the spandex, and yanked him off his bike. The bike didn't even fall. Jesus leaped onto it while it was still wobbling, and the distance between us doubled in seconds.

"He's headed for the bridge," Pete said. The Burnside Bridge is over a thousand feet long, flat, simple, no tolls. No pretension in Portland. So Jesus was headed downtown, no doubt to try to lose us in the warren of one-way streets, MAX trains, and pedestrians angry at the fossil fuel I was burning. If he was lucky, they would swarm my truck like zombies to protest my gas guzzling. Our best bet was to stop him now, but he was too fast. He wove in and out of the cars on Burnside like a needle through cloth.

As we sped toward downtown, we caught a sudden break. The bridge was in motion, the counterweights dropping. I stopped in the line of cars. For the first time ever, I was thankful to miss the bridge. The drop from the bridge to the water is about sixty feet, and they sometimes have to lift it so that boats headed up the Willamette River can get past. Jesus sped past the flashing barriers. Pete jumped out of the car and shouted at me to follow. I paused at the flashing lights and debated, but Pete's lumbering form was already halfway to Jesus.

Jesus turned, trapped against the rising ramp of the bridge. He settled into a kung fu stance as Pete waded toward him. Without warning, Jesus turned and ran up the ramp. Pete tried to follow him, but the incline was getting too steep. Jesus managed to make it all the way to the lamppost sticking out of the bridge just as Pete slid back to the bottom. Jesus held on to the lamppost as it went horizontal.

"We'll catch him when the bridge lowers again," Pete said.

Jesus looked down at me, his smile replaced with a stern glare. "You shouldn't doubt me. You'll regret this. You should respect me as your master!"

"We'll talk all about it when the bridge lowers," I yelled. "And about this parking ticket!" I shook my fist at him.

Jesus laughed. And then he let go of the lamppost and fell. Pete and I surged toward him. He fell like a rock past the deck of the bridge and into the water below. Pete and I ran to the edge, and we could see his blue sash floating away with the current. We ran to the other side of the bridge and saw him pop out of the water like a float. He stepped up on top of the water and turned around to wave at us, laughing. "See you later, Apostle Paul!"

Pete growled. "PETER! I'M PETER!"

Jesus turned and walked south against the flow of the river. We watched him until he walked up on the far shore and climbed onto one of the faux docks for the downtown apartment complexes. Pete's shoulders slumped. Traffic had started again behind us, and people honked enthusiastically at my truck, doors thrown open, empty, the engine running but useless.

"He totally walked on water," I said. "That was cool."

Pete shook his head. "Have you even *met* Jesus before? That guy wasn't even close."

"Of course I have," I snapped. To be honest, Pete had hurt my feelings. "I've been going to church since I was a kid. I've been trying to follow Jesus for as long as I can remember."

Pete sighed. "I guess I didn't know him very well either. Not at the beginning." He looked at me. "I think we need to have a talk if we're going to be able to catch this guy. I'm going to need to tell you my story, and I'll need to hear yours, too."

We got into the truck, and Pete slammed his door. "And if you see a liquor store, pull over," he said. "I have the feeling we're going to need some alcohol."

CHAPTER TWO

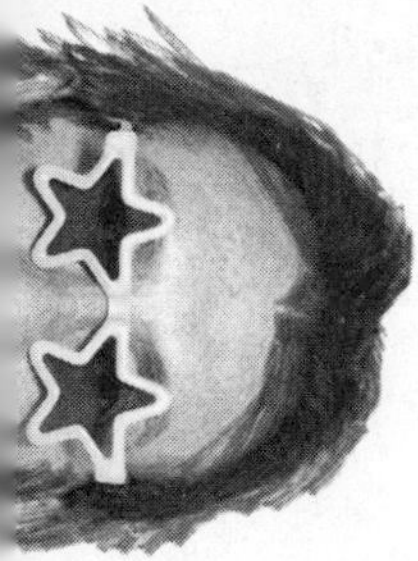

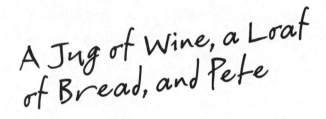

A Jug of Wine, a Loaf of Bread, and Pete

I've never been a drinker. I mean never. I've always told people, "Alcoholism runs in my family." But the fact is, I've never been sure whether Jesus would approve or not. And I get sick of alcoholic Christians trying to convince me that I should guzzle beer with them because we're all "free in Christ." Their insecurity turns them into Bible-thumpers when it comes to the question of alcohol. Jesus' first miracle was turning water into wine, they say. Paul told Timothy to drink wine at night for his stomach. Lot got drunk and had sex with his daughters. Compelling arguments. I find it a lot easier to sit back and say, "Hey, I don't care if you drink. No problem. I abstain for genetic reasons, not religious reasons." Saves time, saves face. And let's be honest, here in Portland several bars are kept in business by Christians with tiny goatees and C. S. Lewis pipes. I guess they feel like they're getting away with something.

Pete made me stop at Trader Joe's on the way home, and he bought a bottle of wine and some flatbread. I live in Vancouver, just north of Portland. As you cross the Columbia River, an inexplicable transformation takes place. Crazy, liberal, free-spirited Portland becomes reasonable, conservative, uptight Vancouver. All the organic restaurants with tiny servings and sidewalk gardens are replaced with "quantity restaurants." I have two restaurants within walking distance of my house with the word *fat* in them: Fatty Patty's and Fat Dave's. Fatty Patty's has a breakfast called the Barnyard that's so huge it has to be served on a cookie sheet. I am not kidding.

We got home, and my wife and daughters were out somewhere. It was Thursday, so that would argue for ballet lessons, I think. I was glad because I wasn't sure how to explain what was going on. "Hi, honey, this is someone claiming to be the apostle Peter. I met him when he was fighting Jesus at our favorite communist café."

We live in a typical two-story tract home on a tenth of an acre. We have a master bathroom smaller than most people's closets, and the kids share the bonus room. But there's more than enough space, about five hundred square feet per person. I parked on the side of the house. As we walked through the grass toward the front porch, Pete stepped in something.

"Sorry about that," I said. "One of the neighbors' dogs has been sneaking into our yard. Sometimes into our backyard, even when the fence is locked. I call him Houdini Dog because I haven't seen him yet, not once. But I often find evidence of his presence." I had spent hours trying to catch this dog in the act, but I couldn't even catch a glimpse of him. He was my canine nemesis.

"No problem," Pete grunted, wiping his shoes in the grass.

When we got into the house, Pete walked into the kitchen and started rummaging through cabinets until he came up with two glasses and a platter. He poured the wine and threw the flatbread onto the plate. Pete took a big drink of the wine, and we sat at the kitchen table. "Nice chairs," he said.

"My father-in-law made them. Windsor chairs, they're called. He cuts down the trees, steams the wood, uses milk paint on them, the whole deal. Pretty amazing."

"I can respect that. Jesus is like that. Loves to work with his hands."

"How can you say that?" I asked. "Because Joseph was a carpenter? How do you come up with that?"

Pete snorted and broke a piece of flatbread in half. "How do you know your sister's favorite flavor of cake?"

"Funfetti, it's called. I just remember it. From when we were kids, I guess."

Chewing on his bread, Pete said, "Jesus is a real person. He has real likes and dislikes. Likes fish, not as fond of lamb. Likes some colors better than others. It happens that he likes to work with his hands. Clay, wood, whatever. I don't 'come up with it.' I know him and I know what he likes."

He pushed a glass of wine in front of me and told me to drink. "I don't," I said.

"Fine with me. Now. If we're going to find your imaginary Jesus, I'll need to ask you a question or two to figure out if you even know the real Jesus."

I sighed. "It seems to me that you could just show me the real one and the fake one would disappear."

Pete looked at me steadily. "If you never confront the imaginary Jesus, he'll keep popping up, perverting what you know about the real Jesus. You need to look him in the face, recognize that he's fake, and renounce him."

I shrugged. "Okay, fine. Ask your questions."

Pete smiled. "If you were sitting down with someone and had five minutes to explain how to follow Jesus, what would you say?"

I sat back in my chair. Believe it or not, this was a pretty easy question for me. "First, I'd tell them that God loves them. And Jesus is God."

Pete nodded. "Go on."

"Then I'd explain how we're all sinful, and we can't get to God."

"Yeah."

"I'd tell them how Jesus is the only way to God. And that he died so we could be with God." Pete had set his cup down and was watching me with strange, unblinking eyes. "And he came back to life," I added hurriedly.

"Okay," Pete said. One of his huge hands wandered aimlessly in front of him on the table, picking at the tablecloth.

"And you have to pray to Jesus to say that you believe all this and you want to follow him."

Pete stood and walked to the sliding glass door. He was staring out at our garden. Krista loves to garden, and she tends the most amazing explosion of color and vegetables in one corner of our yard every year. Dahlias, sunflowers, tomatoes, purple snap beans. But now that winter was coming, the sunflowers were falling and we had culled the beans. You could see the hard work we'd put into it, but it had a tired look, like the life was leeching out of it.

Pete leaned against the glass, resting his forehead on one bent arm. "I don't disagree with anything you say," he said. "But do you know what it looks like when Jesus walks up to someone and says, 'Follow me'? When I first started to follow him, I didn't know that he was God. I didn't know he was the only way to God. I didn't pray to say that I believed it with all my heart. None of that."

I cleared my throat and turned the wineglass in front of me. "You weren't a Christian yet, that's all."

Pete turned, a broad grin on his face. "I disagree, my friend. I strongly disagree." He picked up his glass and took a drink. "I want to show you something. Take a sip of your wine."

"I don't think so," I said. "I'm not taking orders from imaginary people anymore."

Pete's eyebrows shot up. "I'm not imaginary." He picked up the bread and tore off another chunk. "I noticed your imaginary Jesus didn't eat anything at the restaurant." He filled his mouth with bread. "I eat, just like you."

"So you're *real*." I raised a skeptical eyebrow.

"Let's just say that I'm both alive and active," Pete said, grinning and flexing his muscles. "But we're off topic." He walked over to me and bent in close, the smell of fish and sweat infused with wine now. "If I were to take a swipe at you with an imaginary sword, friend, what would you do?"

I nervously scooted my chair back a few inches. "Laugh. And. Um. Feel uncomfortable?"

He grabbed my chair. "No. An imaginary sword that causes real wounds. How would you defend yourself?"

"An imaginary shield."

"That's right." Pete clapped me on the shoulder. "Well said, my friend." He lifted my wine and held it to my lips. "Drink up."

I tried to lean back, but I couldn't get away from him. I closed my eyes and took a sip.

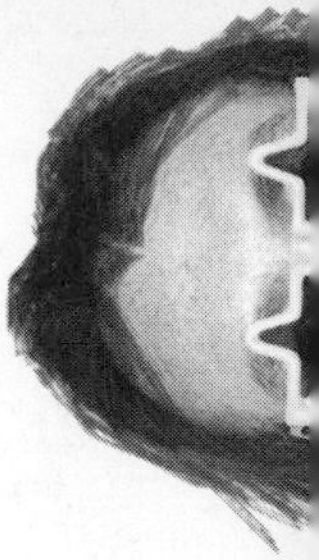

CHAPTER THREE

Imaginary Gardens with Real Toads in Them

I opened my eyes and found myself in Flying Colors. That's the name of the comic book store I worked at ten years ago. The same glass door stood at the entrance, smeared with ice cream from countless faces and hands, the consequence of being next door to Baskin-Robbins. A glassed-in counter full of cards held the cash register, and aisles of four-color comics stretched toward the back of the place, where the rarer comics perched on the wall, stretching up toward the ceiling. Books, ink, toys. A revolving rack of kids' comics up front, walls full of graphic novels. One of the best comic book shops in the world.

"My robot!" I said. Standing next to the register was my little windup robot, his tiny silver body, dome head, and red feet ready to be wound up and sent into action. No one was in the store. I picked it up and showed it to Pete. "When Joe, my boss, did television commercials, I always snuck this little guy into them."

Pete nodded and picked up an issue of *Superman* and flipped through it. "This is the closest thing I could find in your memories to an understanding of what it means to be invited to follow someone."

Just then I saw the Frog of Hate. I grabbed the little plastic frog and held it up triumphantly. "The FROG OF HATE!" How I loved the Frog of Hate. He was a little green frog with a yellow belly. On his stomach in Magic Marker we had written the word *HATE* and drawn an arrow pointed toward his mouth. I showed it to Pete. "Did you ever work retail?" He shook his head. "When customers were driving us crazy, we would take the Frog of Hate and set it out on the register. If they really drove us nuts, we'd make him turn and follow them with his beady little eyes." I cupped him in my hands. "And on rare occasions, when the hate grew to be too much, we would offer to let someone hold him."

I had forgotten how much fun the Hate Club was. A pleasant glow of valued memories shone off the frog. I slipped him into my pocket. Sweet, sweet Frog of Hate.

You are probably wondering why I didn't immediately fall into a pile of gibbering confusion upon taking a sip of wine and opening my eyes to find myself ten years into my own past, standing in a comic book store. You have to understand that a comic book store is a nexus of weirdness. You come to expect that perhaps a dimensional rift will tear open and suck you into it, and you'll find yourself fighting a giant worm bent on universal domination. That's just the sort of thing comic book fans are trained to anticipate. So a little dissociative vision after a sip of wine, that's squaresville, baby. No big deal.

Okay, I was freaking out. "Where are we, Pete?"

"Imaginary gardens," he said, "with real toads in them."

"Marianne Moore."

"Yeah. I've used your imagination to kick-start a memory of yours. It should start up in a minute."

I grabbed a plastic eyeball from a container on the counter and rolled it down the aisle. I wondered idly where the Spock doll was hiding and whether I could sneak some Spawn stickers onto someone's car or something while no one was around. "You can do that?"

"You're so afraid of your imagination," Pete said. "You never use it for good things because you're worried you'll end up imagining something pornographic. You need to get control of yourself. The imagination can be purified like any other part of you."

Just then Sam walked in. Shorter than me, dark hair, olive skin. People sometimes thought we were brothers. He had a wit I lacked and a deep bitterness that made him a favorite among the coworkers. Like some World War II sergeant in a comic book. We knew he was so tough on us because deep down he loved us. So to show our love, we would torture him and one another in return. Strange social misfits often wandered in, and sometimes one of them fixated on one of us. For me it was Hercules Guy, who came in with his creepy, greasy, long hair and would tell me about his collection of Hercules paraphernalia. He never bothered anyone else. But me he would corner.

"I have a sword from episode thirty-five," he would say.

"I just don't care," I would say.

"I have a signed *Xena: Warrior Princess* script," he would say.

"Please, God, make it stop," I would say.

Sam's "Hercules Guy" was Ruth. She came into the store looking for him all the time. We would tell her when he worked so she could drop by and surprise him. And when she came in, we would politely step away so they could have some alone time. One time she came in to show Sam pictures from her open-heart surgery. Pictures! Sam stood at the counter in mute horror as we watched from the back of the store. For some inexplicable reason she loved him and wanted to share her life with him.

Now, Sam stood behind the counter, flipping through a comic book.

"You're on." Pete nudged me forward.

"What do you mean?"

"I mean, you better get up there next to him. Ruth is about to walk in."

The door swung open and Ruth did just that. She was dumpy, overweight, and she wore baggy, mismatched clothes. She walked straight to Sam. I stood beside him behind the counter, boxes of reserved comics behind us at our feet, the phone hanging on the wall, the Frog of Hate in my pocket.

"Sam," she said, her round face quivering with emotion. "I've come to say good-bye."

Sam looked up from his comic, his face filled with wonder. He gave a mighty effort to keep the glee from showing on his face. "Good-bye? Why good-bye, Ruth?"

Ruth rummaged through her purse and flattened a piece of crumpled paper on the counter. She looked around the store, giving me a long glance and leaning toward Sam to make it clear the conversation wasn't for me. I set a *Starman* comic book on the counter and pretended to look at it. "On August 28th," she said in a low voice, "Atlantis will rise from the sea." This pronouncement of weird shook me and Sam. Even for a comic book store, this was an exceptional moment of the profoundly bizarre. "There will be tidal waves. The entire western seaboard will be destroyed."

Sam leaned toward her despite himself, and I found that I, too, was eager to hear what strange tidings she bore. She quickly sketched out a map on the piece of paper, filling in highways and cross streets and circling a spot in Montana. "This ranch in Montana will be safe." She grabbed hold of Sam's hand, and he was so surprised that he didn't flinch. "If you come with me, Sam, you'll be safe. I'll be waiting for you." She let go of his hand and ran out the door, sobbing.

Sam, shell-shocked, reached mechanically for the map and held it in trembling hands. I moved closer to him, and together we studied it in silent fascination. "So," I said, and Sam tore his gaze from the map and looked up at me. "Are you going on a trip?"

Without a smile or hint of amusement, Sam looked at me and spoke with complete certainty. "I would rather drown." He folded the map, opened the drawer in front of him, and stuck the paper in the Stupid Book, the place where we recorded the extremes of human folly that presented themselves to us at Flying Colors. Sam went on break soon after that, and Pete came up to the counter, a giant pile of comics between his meaty paws.

"Spire comics." Pete held one up. "Strange comic book adaptations of Christian books from the seventies. I kind of like them."

"I had that *Cross and the Switchblade* one when I was a kid," I said. "I liked it. Not as much as *Spider-Man* or anything, though." I started ringing Pete up. "Thirty-five cents apiece back in the seventies, Pete. Can you believe that? Didn't cost much back then."

"How much would it have cost Sam to go with Ruth?"

"Everything, I guess. He would have had to quit his job, leave all his stuff. If he really believed her, anyway. Oh, hey, I didn't know there was a Johnny Cash comic."

"And she made an implicit promise of relationship to Sam."

"But he didn't want that." I paused, a copy of the 1979 *Jesus* comic by Al Hartley in my hand. I flipped it open to the first page, where a bearded man and his friends listened to Jesus—a Jesus who looked a lot like my imaginary Jesus, but with a red sash—commanding that they throw in their nets. The bearded man looked like a Caucasian, whitewashed version of Pete. I showed it to him. "Is that you?" I laughed. "Jesus just walks up and shows you some fish and you ditch your boat and follow him?"

Pete took the comic book from me and looked at it for a long time, a smile twitching at the ends of his lips. "That's not how it happened," he said. "Not at all." He looked up at me. "We should be on our way. Your imaginary Jesus has quite a head start on us."

"Where are we going?"

"I have a friend named Daisy with exceptional spiritual discernment. I'd like to introduce you."

"I don't want to leave Flying Colors, though."

He pointed at the door. Hercules Guy was pushing it open. "Matt!" he said. *Oh, please. Not this guy.* I closed my eyes.

When I opened them again I was standing on a dusty, crowded street. People rushed by in Universal Studios Moses outfits. Donkeys. Chickens. Stalls selling fish. "Please tell me this isn't ancient Judea," I said to Pete. But when I looked around, Pete wasn't there.

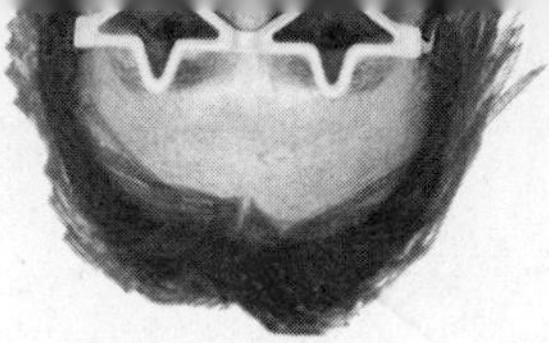

CHAPTER FOUR

In One Year and Out the Other

The first century smelled like what Christians call a "men's retreat." This is when men leave their wives and children for several days, go to the mountains, and yell at each other, "Stop neglecting your wife and children!" The unique stench of a men's retreat comes from the close company of men at high altitude eating only beans, steak, and onions, combined with a lack of bathing and shaving. The entire first-century culture revolved around the men's retreat concept. Every man in sight sported a beard that doubled as a napkin, and you could close your eyes and smell where each person was standing. The main difference between the first century and a twenty-first-century men's retreat was that all the men here wore dresses. Scratchy, modest dresses.

I did a 360 looking for Pete. I saw a synagogue, a donkey tied to a post, a crowded market street, a synagogue again, a donkey again, and then I stopped. I suspected that the people around me spoke Aramaic or Hebrew, and not English, which I knew hadn't been invented yet. I racked my brain for any trace of Aramaic and came up with something. I grabbed a man walking by and said, *"Eloi, Eloi, lama sabachthani."*

He jumped, his eyes wide and his beard quivering, and pulled his arm away. "If you're going to live in Judea, you ought to learn the language."

"Oh, good," I said, "you speak . . . uh . . . the same language as me." But he was gone by then. I tried to act like I belonged by leaning against the post where the donkey was tied up. She looked like a local. She stared at me with her big black eyes. She appeared friendly enough, with her dusty brown fur and a white star on her muzzle. I asked her, "You seen a guy named Pete around here anywhere?"

"I think you hurt his feelings," the donkey said.

I gasped. "Good grief. The apostle Peter totally drugged me." I figured if the donkey could talk, maybe the post could too. "Did you hear that donkey speak to me?" The post didn't say anything. But posts are known for being stuck-up.

"Are you talking to that *post*?" the donkey asked.

"Yeah," I said. "Are you a talking donkey?"

The donkey blew a raspberry out through her lips. "You tell me, smart guy. My name is *Bellis Perennis*, but you can call me Daisy. Pete sent me here to help you out."

"I assumed that Daisy would be a, uh, person."

The donkey snorted. "Well, you know what assuming does. Look, you're going to be back in Portland soon, Matt, so you don't have much time. You need to walk into the synagogue over there, because Y'shua is about to give a speech. Pete wants you to see it."

"Y'shua, like Jesus?"

"Right."

The thought of walking into the synagogue made me feel out of place. I wasn't even Jewish. I couldn't remember how to cross myself or where the holy water was or anything. I felt awkward, like a fourteen-year-old on his first date with a real live girl. "Could you come in with me?" Daisy stared up at me with her big black eyes and furry face as if to say, *No donkeys in the synagogue*. Fine then, I would do it myself.

I walked into the synagogue and took a place toward the back, crowded in with the other men. The man standing in front held out his hand and was given a scroll. He was short, balding, dark-skinned, and hunched over. His mouth was far too wide, like a frog's. He wore a brown robe, covered in dirt. I kept looking around for Jesus, but I didn't see him anywhere. The man's dark eyes flashed over the words on the scroll, and he held it high before the men gathered in the room.

I leaned over to the guy next to me. "Have you seen a teacher named Y'shua around here?" He pointed to the bent man in front of us with his chin. "That's not him," I said, outraged. His face was thin, little more than skin laid on bone. He looked unhealthy. He looked weak.

"He's been fasting in the wilderness," the man next to me explained. "Alone but for the adversary and the angels and the Spirit of God."

As if on cue, the man began to read. "'The Spirit of Adonai is on me, because the Lord has chosen me to bring good news to the poor.'" He paused here and looked down to the scroll, a smile curling up from his too-wide lips. "'He has sent me to repair the brokenhearted. He has sent me to tell the slaves that they are free. He has sent me to release the prisoners from their darkness and to *proclaim* . . . !'" He raised his voice, and we all gasped, leaning in to hear his next words. "'To proclaim the year of the Lord's *favor*.'" The way he savored the word made me want it desperately—the Lord's favor. God's approval or well-wishes or whatever it meant, I knew it was something good. Although the twisted little man didn't move, it was as if he were walking among us, placing his hands on our shoulders, speaking to us individually. He opened his mouth as if to speak another word, but then he rolled up the scroll and handed it back to the attendant. I wanted to shout, "More!" I wanted him to explain what it meant. But he simply said, "The words of this prophecy have been fulfilled today, while you listened." Then he stepped down from the platform and took his seat.

No sermon followed. The words from the scroll bounced around in my head, looking for a place to perch. The crowd of men burst out of the synagogue, carrying me along with them. I kept looking over my shoulder, trying to get another look at the man. He read the Scripture so that it spoke without commentary. He acted like he understood what he read, as if the meaning was plain to see and meant to be understood by any one of us. At the same time I couldn't wrap my mind around the fact that this strange little man might actually be Jesus. He simply didn't match my picture of Jesus and the internal dissonance was giving me a headache.

I walked over to the donkey at the post. "So you're telling me that ugly guy was Jesus."

The donkey didn't say anything. I looked at her more closely. Or rather, him. Good grief, someone stole my talking donkey. A man carrying a crate full of chickens was walking by. "Excuse me, sir, have you seen a donkey?"

"Yes," the man said. "Many times."

"What I mean is, have you seen *my* donkey?"

The man stopped, looked around, and then pointed to the donkey beside me. "There is a donkey."

"That's not my donkey," I told him, "but I left her tied up right here."

The man stroked his beard. "Are there any distinguishing characteristics of your donkey, sir, which might help us ascertain her whereabouts?"

I looked carefully at the chickens. Was it possible that they could help me more than this man? Could they perhaps be talking chickens? I decided no. And let's be honest, if chickens could talk, they would be very hard to understand due to the fact that they have no lips.

"She is a girl donkey named Daisy," I said.

"Yes?"

"She was tied to this post."

"And?"

"And she can talk. Like a person."

The man bowed his head politely. "I assure you, sir, that if I come across a talking donkey, you will be the first to know." Then he walked quickly away.

So there I was, lost in first-century Judea. No apostle and no talking donkey. I thought about praying for help, but I was concerned about praying to ugly Jesus, and also concerned that God might be mad at me for drinking the wine, which Peter had apparently spiked. I had just about decided to lie down in the street and wait for the wine to wear off when I saw a familiar face moving into the market. It was Pete! Younger, thinner, and wearing a scratchy dress, which was apparently all the rage this century.

I ran up to him and grabbed him by the shoulders. "There you are, Pete! I was getting worried!"

Pete pulled away from me. "That's not my name," he said gruffly. "You've confused me with someone else."

"Ha-ha. What a prankster you are."

"Excuse me." Pete pushed me away and walked deeper into the market. "I need to find a physician."

"Hey," I called after him, "if you see a talking donkey, she's *mine*!"

CHAPTER FIVE

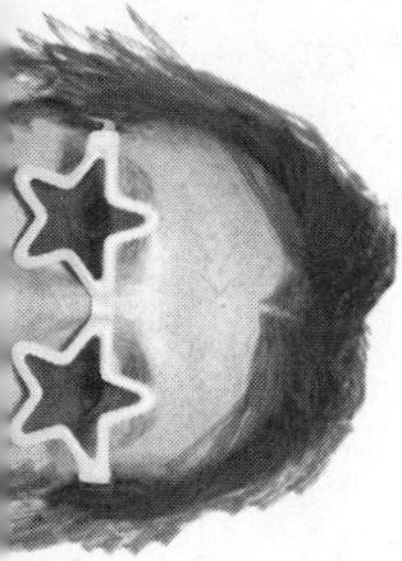

A Doctor in the House

There's an entire genre of Christian cartoons and kids' radio shows where plucky, well-meaning children are transported to the first century so that they can help the bumbling wise men find baby Jesus. It's clearly an important place in the space-time continuum, because kids are always finding magic books, Christmas tree ornaments, and flying carpets that whisk them away to Judea so that Jesus can give them a quick lecture on morality.

I started looking for white kids in T-shirts and shorts. I didn't have a solid plan, but I thought maybe I could snatch their magic book and fly it back home. I didn't like the first century. It was hot. It stank. I couldn't find the bathroom. And my tour guide, the talking donkey, had abandoned me. Whether by her own design or because an evil merchant sold her to a circus, I wasn't sure.

Vendors sold fish, bolts of cloth, and spices. A donkey brayed, but not in English. Chickens ran around my feet. The chickens appeared to be in control of things, walking in and out of houses with impunity. Sort of like cats in our century.

The only person I knew in the entire world was young Pete. I tried to follow him without being obvious. He had an intense conversation with a friend about getting a physician, and then he hurried down an alley while his friend ran the other direction.

Pete led me through a mess of interweaving streets. He looked nervous, and he moved so fast that I had a hard time keeping up. At last he turned in at a flat-roofed, whitewashed home. Modest, I was guessing. Not much different than mine maybe, just in another century.

I waited outside for about ten minutes. Some sort of stinging fly kept biting me in the neck. I killed it. But then its many relatives tried to take their revenge. I slapped at them and thought evil thoughts about them until I couldn't take it anymore. I strode up to Pete's front door and knocked. A beautiful young woman answered the door, her cheeks flushed, her dark hair matted to the sides of her face. The intense look of worry in her eyes relaxed slightly when she saw me, and she immediately stepped back to let me into the house.

"Come in, Doctor." I turned around and looked behind me, but I didn't see a doctor. "This way," she said. "My mother is getting worse by the moment. She won't speak any longer."

I followed her into a back room, and the first thing that hit me was the sour smell of death. I had only smelled it before hidden under the cold, antiseptic scents of hospitals. The woman was sunk into the bed, her wrinkled face twisted in agony. I could feel the heat coming off her. The young woman perched on the edge of the bed, wiping her mother's face with a cloth.

Pete stepped out of a corner of the room, giving me a quizzical look. "You're the doctor?"

I cleared my throat. I thought about it and decided that as a twenty-first-century man, I was better than any primitive doctor they might get. "Yes," I said. I stepped closer to the sick woman. I put my hand on her forehead and she groaned and turned away from me. Her head radiated heat and I yanked my hand from her, covered in her sweat. I suddenly realized that she could have bubonic plague. Was that in the first century? What was the most deadly contagious disease I could catch by being in this room? I cursed myself for not paying more attention in my History of Contagious Diseases class. Actually, I never took that class. That now appeared to have been a dangerous oversight.

"Have you given her aspirin?"

Pete and the young woman exchanged glances. "I don't know what that is," the woman said.

"It's like Tylenol." They stared at me blankly. "Advil."

Pete gasped and the woman shrieked. "Forgive us, Doctor," Pete said. He grabbed her hand. "But did you say that my mother-in-law has a *devil*?"

"What?" The ragged breathing of the woman on the bed drew my attention. "No!" Then again, thinking back on my Bible reading, it seemed like demon-possessed people were all over the place. My experience in that arena had been spotty at best. I hoped she was just sick. "She has a fever."

"What kind of fever?" Pete asked.

"A . . . uh . . . *high* fever."

Pete pulled on his thick black beard nervously. "What can we do?"

I took a deep breath. And then I thought maybe I'd just inhaled a billion bacteria. Or viruses. My heart sped up. I thought maybe I had a fever. Also, the lack of a medicine cabinet had quickly exhausted my superior medical know-how.

Now this lady was going to die because her doctor from the future had no Advil with him. Then a spectacular flash of genius came upon me. "Ice. Get me some ice."

Pete's wife frowned. "It's the middle of summer, Doctor. Where will we get ice?"

"From the refrig—er—never mind." I pushed my hair back and sighed. "Leave me alone with her for a few minutes."

Pete and his wife backed out of the room. It looked like the young woman was about to start crying. I closed the door and leaned my head against it. This woman was going to die, and then I would contract the Ebola virus from being locked in this room and I would die here too. And I was guessing that the burial rituals would make me uncomfortable, even if I was dead already. A chicken would probably walk across my corpse. Was there no dignity in this century?

"Need some help?"

I recognized that voice. I turned and saw him standing by the bed, a big grin on his face and a bottle of aspirin in his nail-scarred hands. Imaginary Jesus. I felt the sudden burn of anger in my face. At least, I hoped it was a burn of anger and not a fever. "Yeah, I need your help," I said. "It seems that I somehow got a *parking ticket* in Portland today."

Jesus waved me off. "Let's focus on the issues of the moment, Mikalatos. Do you want this aspirin for the lady or not?"

My hand hovered between my body and the aspirin, fluttering indecisively like a hummingbird between a bird feeder and a flower. Then it struck, grabbed the little plastic container, and struggled to open it.

"I knew you'd come back to me," Jesus said.

"Curse these child safety caps!" I strained at it with superhuman strength. An explosion of white pills rained down on the room, rolling under the bed, covering the blankets, scattering over the woman's face. I frantically started scooping them up and tried to get them back into the bottle.

"Do you think I just destroyed the space-time continuum?"

Jesus shrugged. "I doubt it."

"But what if someone sees the pills and they figure out how aspirin works and then they invent it too early and that somehow saves Hitler's life and he ends up winning World War II?"

"You read too much science fiction," Jesus said.

I tried to get a pill into the sick woman's mouth, but she thrashed weakly and all that happened was that I got hot saliva on my fingers. I grabbed five aspirin and downed them, just to be safe.

The door swung open and Pete and his wife walked in, followed by the misshapen man from the synagogue. "This is Y'shua," Pete said. "We had invited him for dinner, and I've asked him to look at my mother-in-law."

Y'shua's dark, calm eyes found mine, and he seemed amused to see me. His wide mouth curled up on one side into a lopsided smile. But when he saw my Jesus standing behind me, the smile disappeared and his thick eyebrows drew down toward the center of his face.

He bent over the bed and cupped the woman's face in one hand. "Simon," the daughter said, pulling on her husband's arm. "Maybe we shouldn't disturb her. She isn't well."

Y'shua leaned over the sick woman and spoke directly to her, or so it seemed. He spoke sternly, his voice slightly raised and firm, and ordered the fever to go away. The woman relaxed and let out a deep sigh, her muscles unclenching, her face smoothing. She opened her eyes and looked into his. The temperature of the room dropped, as if a cool fall wind had drawn the sickness away.

"I'll make dinner," she said, and began to sit up. Her daughter took hold of her shoulders and urged her to stay in bed, but she shrugged her off. "We have a guest. Let me make the teacher a meal, dear."

Jesus took her hands solemnly. "Thank you, madam," he said.

Pete, a look of astonishment on his face, pulled me aside to say that I was welcome to stay but no longer needed. I looked around for Imaginary Jesus, thinking he might be able to take me home to the U. S. of A., but he was gone again.

When we walked into the front room, a few of the neighbors stuck their heads in to ask what had happened. "Y'shua rebuked the fever," Pete informed them, "and it disappeared."

Pete's mother-in-law appeared, dressed and cheerful, and waved to the neighbors. She set about making the kitchen ready and sent her daughter back to the market. "A feast," she whispered, "not just a meal. Spare no expense."

Within an hour the house was packed, overflowing into the street. People perched on the windowsills, crowded around the table, and sat on the floor, and Y'shua stood on the hearth, sweat rolling down his dark face while he taught. He prayed for an old man with a twisted leg and it straightened until he dropped his staff. Another man brought in his little girl, who spat and cursed, her eyes rolling back into her head. A path cleared in the sea of people, and Y'shua walked through it and took hold of the girl and said, “Come out of her.” She shook and fell to the ground, and Pete carried her to the bedroom, where his wife brought her water. The girl’s father stroked her face, weeping. It had been years, he said, since he had seen his little girl without the demon in her.

Night came. The moon rose and then slid into the sea. People flowed in and out again. Sick people arrived and well people left. The lamps flickered, and in the darkness his voice came to us, round and sure, a light purer than anything else in the room. A few fell asleep listening to him talk. People brought their children to see the teacher. Men and women alike crowded into the little house. And then the sun cracked the edifice of night, and light and color flooded the house, the golden light of morning.

Somehow in the morning light, Jesus slipped away. At first people didn’t notice. The teacher had taken a well-deserved break. But after a time, a few people went outside searching for him, and then a few more. Others hung around the house, hoping he would return.

I walked outside, still trying to figure out where they kept the bathrooms. I had to go, and bad. That’s when the donkey said, “Psssst. Over here.”

CHAPTER SIX

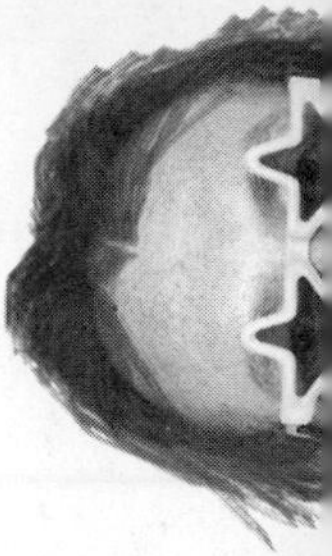

Matt Mikalatos, Donkey Disciple

"Where *were* you?" I hissed. "Was there an emergency load of sticks that had to be hauled or something?"

Daisy rolled her eyes. "You think you're the only thing I have going this week?"

"Where are the bathrooms in this place?"

"I'm a theologian, not a human sociologist," the donkey answered.

"I'm too embarrassed to ask anyone."

"Walk with me. Pete's down at the lakeside, and he wants to see you."

The crisp morning air felt great, and I could smell the water, a welcome change for my nose. Daisy said, "Pete tells me that when you two spoke earlier, you made it sound like Y'shua hypnotized him. Pete didn't follow Y'shua because of the fish." She paused for a moment on the road. "God had seemed silent for hundreds of years, and then a prophet showed up in Pete's living room and healed his mother-in-law. And Y'shua taught in a way that Pete had never seen before."

"You know a lot for a donkey," I said. I could see the lake

now, flat, wide, and beautiful. A few boats moved across the face of it, and the beach stretched out, inviting and pleasant. "Is that why Pete became his disciple—because he wanted to know how to read the Scriptures like Jesus?"

Daisy paused. "Do you understand what it means to be someone's disciple?"

I thought about it and absently kicked at a chicken pecking at my feet. It was like a plague of chickens. "I thought it meant 'student.'"

"Yes, but not how you think of it. You're thinking of Y'shua like an algebra teacher. But to be a disciple means more than *learning*. It means to become like your teacher. It means transformation from what I am into what my teacher is. Y'shua said once, 'Everyone who is fully trained will *be like* his teacher.'"

"So you're saying that if I was, for instance, your disciple—"

"You wouldn't need to find a bathroom," the donkey said, "because we're walking on a perfectly fine road. You would eat when I eat, you would rest when I rest, and under the same olive tree. You wouldn't take the shortcut while I went the long way. We would be inseparable. You would live like my shadow, mimicking my actions until you could do what I do without thinking, until you had the same instincts, thoughts, and words."

As we neared the water's edge I saw a huge crowd gathered near two fishermen's boats. The crooked man sat in one of the boats, along with Peter and the other fishermen. His face had thickened, and he looked stronger. Still not the Jesus I knew. I couldn't see any reason people would be drawn to him, at least no physical reason. He was ugly. But the people pressed near him as if he were a movie star.

"That's not how Jesus really looked, is it?"

"Humans all look the same to me. Does it matter?"

"I'm not sure," I said. In fact, it disturbed me deeply. Jesus shouldn't be an ugly, twisted man. He should be compelling, beautiful, and charismatic. He should look like a president. He should look like JFK in a robe. He should look like my imaginary Jesus.

Jesus sat in the bow and taught the people. They sat on the shore. One man waded into the water so that he could hear better, unconcerned about how ridiculous he looked. Children laughed and played behind their parents. People coughed and murmured to one another. Occasionally someone would shout a question and Jesus would answer.

Toward the end of his teaching, Jesus gestured to the nets laid out on the shore. "The Kingdom of Heaven is like a net that was let down into the lake and caught all sorts of fish." Pete's face burned at that, and his men frowned. Apparently they hadn't caught anything the night before. "When it was full, the fishermen pulled the net onto shore, and they sorted the fish. They put the good fish into baskets but threw the bad away." The fishermen nodded. If they had any fish, they would be sorting them right now. "At the end of the age, the angels will come and separate the righteous from the wicked," Jesus continued. "And the wicked will be thrown into the furnace, where they will sob and gnash their teeth."

"Hey," I said to Daisy. "I thought Jesus taught this later. Seems like the chronology is all messed up."

Daisy snorted. "Do you really think he only spoke his parables once and then never taught them again? He taught nearly every day for three years. He often taught the same lessons again, or with slightly different wording."

Jesus turned to Pete. "Put out into deeper water and let down your nets for a catch."

Pete exchanged glances with his fishermen. He spoke in a low tone so his words wouldn't carry across the water, but we heard them just the same. "Master, we've been fishing all night, and we haven't caught anything."

One of the other fishermen said, "The fishing is best at night, Master. It's not a good time for catching fish."

Jesus didn't move, he just watched Pete carefully. Pete stared back. Maybe he was thinking about his mother-in-law, sick in her bed until Jesus spoke. Maybe he was thinking about his whole neighborhood crowded into his house. Pete was the first to look away. He grumbled something under his breath. "But because you say so, I will let down the nets." He called to his men and they launched out into deeper water.

Pete's partner called from the shore, "Simon, what are you doing?" Pete ignored him, and he and his men gathered up the nets and cast them into the water. The entire boat jerked to the side. It looked as if a dinosaur had caught the net and yanked. Pete grabbed the side of the boat and looked into the water.

"What happened?" someone shouted.

"Pull in the nets," Pete said. His men grabbed hold of the nets and pulled, muscles bulging. Fish, thousands of them, churned up the water inside the nets. Jesus sat in the bow, laughing and full of joy.

The boat tipped toward the fish, and water started pouring over the sides and into the boat. Pete yelled, "James, John, bring your boat! Hurry!" His partners ran to their boat and headed out. Meanwhile, the fishermen were pulling fish out of the net and throwing them into the boat. "It's going to break. Get all the fish you can," one of them cried.

The boat was sinking and fish swam around the fishermen's legs. By the time James and John's boat pulled alongside to help, Pete was thigh-deep in water and still sinking. They reached over and started to pull the nets into their boat, and soon they were sinking too. Pete stopped what he was doing and looked at Jesus, perched on the bow of the boat, his broad face split in a wide grin. Pete sloshed over to him and fell to his knees, chest-deep in the water. He grabbed hold of Jesus' knees and said, "Go away from me, Lord. I am a sinful man." He looked back at the fish.

Jesus put his hands on Pete's shoulders. "Don't be afraid, Simon." He pointed back at the astonished fishermen, the fish leaping in the boat, the nets straining to hold what appeared to be every fish in the lake. "Do you see all these fish? If you follow me, I will make you a fisherman who catches *people*." Pete looked into Jesus' eyes, and I saw a flicker of confusion. Pete bit his lip, then turned and began shouting orders to his men. Somehow they managed—exhausted, soaked, and exhilarated—to get the boats back to shore, the net and the fish strung between them.

Jesus jumped from the bow and began walking along the lake again. Some in the crowd followed, and the fishermen started to sort the fish. But Pete stood like a man in a trance. "Come on," he said to his crew. James and John had already started after the teacher.

"But the fish," one of the men protested.

Pete glanced down at them. "The teacher can get more whenever it pleases him." And he walked off, leaving his boats and the nets and the fish behind him.

I turned to follow, but Daisy caught hold of my shirt and I noticed Old Pete sitting on a rock, the cup of wine in his hand. He took a drink and smiled at me.

"That's not the Jesus from the Red and Black Café," I said.

Pete shook his head.

"Let's go." I said. "I want to see what he does next. Forget Imaginary Jesus."

Pete shook his head again. "Have you forgotten what I told you back at your house? Every time you think about Jesus, you picture your imaginary one. For you to see *him*—" he gestured down the beach—"we need to eliminate your imaginary Jesus."

I shrugged. "If you say so. Let's do it." I looked back toward the retreating shape of the ugly Jesus.

"Can I point out one thing to you, friend? Did you notice that in all Y'shua's teachings so far, he had never yet said, 'I am the way and the truth and the life and no one comes to the Father but by me?' Do you see that when I threw down my nets it had nothing to do with eternal life? I wanted to be like that man." He pointed at the teacher. "Pure and simple. I saw his life, not his future. I knew he was an amazing teacher and a person of power, but I didn't know he was God. Not yet. Do you see that?"

"Yeah, I can see why. I would want to be like him too. He's not the Jesus I've seen in a lot of churches. The way he talked about freedom for the oppressed in the synagogue . . . and the healings at your house. The way he teaches is amazing too. I can tell he knows what he's talking about, not just throwing out theories."

Pete said, "Even without the promise of eternal life, I gave up everything to follow him. I didn't know him well. But I knew him well enough."

I kicked over a rock on the sand. "So, what's the next step? How do we find my imaginary Jesus?"

"You ought to look where you usually see him," Daisy suggested. "We could try a church. They hang around there like flies."

Pete shook his head. "Matt's imaginary Jesus is on the run. He's going to be hiding. So the better trick would be to think of places he definitely would *not* be. That's where we start. The question right now, Matt, is where would your Jesus never go?"

I thought about this. There were a lot of places my Jesus didn't like. All-you-can-eat buffets. R-rated movies. Scary neighborhoods at night. But I knew there was one place my Jesus would never go, not in a million years. Not in infinity years, and then some. If I were my imaginary Jesus, this is precisely where I would hide out.

I cleared my throat. I felt a little color creeping up my neck and into my ears. "Um," I said, "with a lady of the night?"

"Like a lady night watchman?" Daisy asked. "Is that what you mean?"

"No, I mean he would never be alone with a prostitute."

"Ah." Pete steepled his fingers like the top of a church. "I wondered when this would come up." He stood. "Come along then, Matt."

"Where are we going?"

"We're off to find a whore."

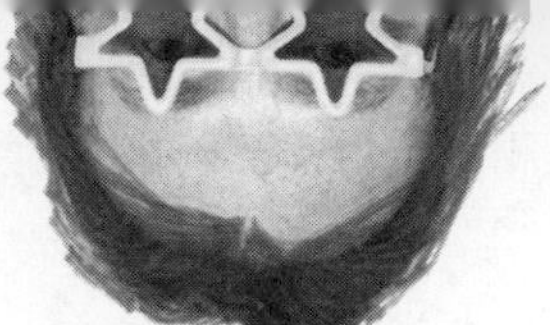

CHAPTER SEVEN

Something's Going On Down the Road over Yonder

You might think that meeting Jesus in the first century would be the climactic moment of a story like this one. But when my eyes fluttered open, I found myself sitting in my own dining room, Pete's cup of wine making a perspiration ring on my wife's table. It felt like an extended hallucination in which I had been more of an observer than a participant. It was like going backstage after a play about Jesus and meeting the actor. But I already knew Jesus' story. . . . I wanted to know more about his role in my own. I didn't feel that Jesus had given me answers. He hadn't even let me ask a question.

Which is why, I guess, Pete and I wedged into the cab of my truck and he directed me to a modest apartment near downtown Portland. Within ten minutes, we sat at the fold-out kitchen table of a former prostitute named Sandy. I told her and Pete that I had—accidentally—picked up a prostitute once before. I was in Seattle, I explained, and had taken the Forty-fifth/Fiftieth Street exit off of Highway 5. It was cold and late at night, and as it happens I was on my way home from helping out with a big Christian meeting with Christian college students.

She was standing on the side of the road, and while I sat at the red light she ran up to the passenger window. When I rolled it down, she said, "Hey, my car ran out of gas, and it's cold out. Could you give me a lift back to my car?"

In retrospect, this question made no sense. *Could you give me a lift back to my car that has no gas?* At the time, it seemed perfectly reasonable. And it was cold. The only issue was that my wife and I had this rule about never being alone with people of the opposite gender, even in a car, ever since our encounter with a woman who disguised herself as a young boy so she could lure youth workers into being alone with her and then blackmail them by saying that they had attacked her. Which is another story entirely. Point is, the family rule said I shouldn't be alone with a woman in my car.

On the other hand, the woman was cold. She was rubbing her arms. The air churned through the window like cubes of ice falling into a glass. "It's just a couple of blocks," she told me, which in retrospect also made no sense, especially when I nodded for her to get in the car and she said, "Get back on the freeway."

She had long, dirty blonde hair and was wearing tight jeans and a puffy parka. She smelled like a hundred cigarettes and car exhaust. I pulled onto the freeway. "What's your name?" she asked.

"Matt."

"John?"

"No, Matt."

"Nice to meet you, John."

Great, I thought, *I just picked up a crazy lady*.

"How far is your car, anyway?" I asked. And then she leaned

over and kissed me on the cheek and thanked me for the ride. As the smell of cigarettes followed her back to her side of the car, a little voice in the back of my head asked, *Don't prostitutes call their customers "johns"?*

My eyes widened in terror. At the same time I felt a deep sense of thankfulness for television cop shows, where I had learned this important piece of slang. Who knows when I would have figured it out otherwise? "Miss," I said, "I'm sorry, but I just figured out what it is you do, and I'm going to need to let you out of the car."

"Oh." She barely paused. "Is it because you're a Christian or something?"

"Yes." I let out a deep breath. Now we understood each other.

She put her hand on my knee. "Relax. I've been with lots of Christians. I've even been with *pastors*."

All the little fight-or-flight critters in my head started sounding the emergency klaxons and sending messengers to my brain: YOU MIGHT HAVE TO FIGHT THIS WOMAN, they said. OR YOU COULD THROW OPEN THE CAR DOOR AND ROLL TO SAFETY. *I am on the highway,* I told them. *That could kill me.* I took a look at her out of the corner of my eye. *And I am pretty sure this woman could take me in a fight.* WE WILL INCREASE YOUR ADRENALINE AND YOU WILL FEEL NO PAIN, they said.

I moved her hand. I pulled off the highway at the next exit and into the parking lot of a bank. "You'll have to get out here." When she didn't move I added, "Sorry."

"How am I going to get to work now, sweetie?"

"Maybe someone else will come along and accidentally give you a ride."

She folded her arms. "I'm not getting out of this car without some money."

"I haven't got any."

"You're the one who picked me up," she insisted, making it clear that this was all my fault.

"I thought you needed a ride to your car."

"Oh, please. Don't be naive."

"That should be much easier after tonight."

"There's a bank right there. Go get some cash."

I suddenly thought of the ATM cameras. Then I imagined the newspapers the next day: "Mikalatos Caught with Prostitute." *Front-page news*, I thought. I wondered if those little ATM cameras could see across the parking lot.

A glance at my empty wallet finally convinced her to get out, and I left her standing alone in the pooled light of a lamppost, shivering and rubbing her arms and shouting after me. I arrived home freaked out, told my wife about it, and couldn't sleep.

Sandy stirred a spoon in her coffee. Her short blonde hair had red tips, and she wore a black, high-necked dress, a green army jacket over it, and knee-high army boots. "So if your Jesus found himself in an awkward position with a woman, he would drive her to the middle of nowhere and abandon her."

I grinned sheepishly. "I guess so. I was panicking."

Pete grunted and took another bite of chocolate pie. "You do have to consider the way it looked, of course. It wasn't wise to pick her up alone in a car."

"He wasn't like that with me," Sandy said. "On the outskirts of the worst part of town, and he struck up a conversation. I told him he shouldn't be talking to someone like me. He just laughed and said I didn't know him very well."

"We found him in a situation like that once, too," Pete said. "Alone and talking with a woman. We were shocked, but we didn't ask him what he was doing. I was afraid of what he might answer."

Sandy nodded. "I tried to throw him off the trail. I threw politics at him, theology, culture—nothing worked. He kept watching me with those big black eyes and I could tell that . . ." Her voice trailed off and she blushed. "I could tell that he *loved* me." She cleared her throat and took a sip of coffee. "He didn't care that people were watching. He didn't stop talking to me. He looked at me in a different way than the johns. As if sex was the farthest thing from his mind."

I still felt a little awkward around Sandy. She had left prostitution behind three years ago, and she went to a church that Pete knew about. She was clean and sober, and she worked downtown at a coffee shop called Stumptown.

"Thanks for helping tonight," I said, and I meant it. "I've never really met a prostitute before, and you're so nice."

She laughed. "We were all whores before we met him." I wasn't sure what she meant, but I didn't ask any questions. I felt awkward about implying that she was still a prostitute and apologized. She laughed and told me to get over it. "I made money from sex. It was my job. It's not glamorous. It's not exciting. You just want the day to be over so you can watch television."

Pete said Sandy knew the streets and the broken-down little apartments out here pretty well, and he trusted her. She still had some friends out this way, and he thought she would be great for getting us around and into the neighborhood where Imaginary Jesus was most likely to be holed up.

"There may be more than one," Pete said.

"More than one neighborhood?" I asked.

"More than one Jesus. They tend to multiply when they're on the run. . . ."

CHAPTER EIGHT

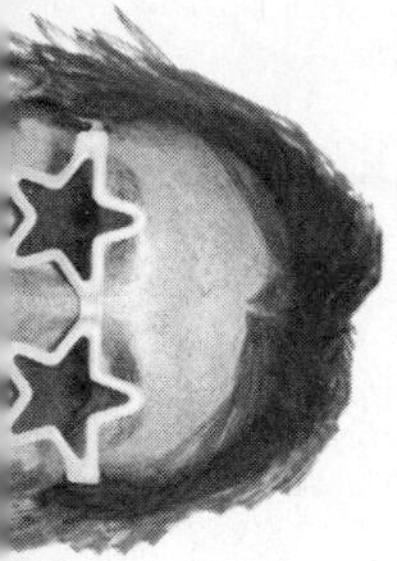

Lamb on the Lam

"Here's the place," Sandy said. It looked like a squalid tenement. I didn't even know there were places like this in Portland, though I suppose every city has them somewhere. "My friends say this place is chock-full of people in hiding. Judy said she saw a couple guys who matched your description of Jesus, Matt. Third floor."

We went in through the front door and heard angry voices coming from down the hall. We walked up the stairs and saw a Jesus in a loincloth with bleeding hands crouched in the stairwell. "Gross," I said, being careful not to touch him as we walked by.

"Some people prefer Jesus mostly dead." Pete stepped over the man like he'd seen this hundreds of times.

"Not dead yet," said the man in the loincloth.

We came to the third floor, and Pete carefully put his ear against several doors. On the fifth one he gave us a thumbs-up. "I'll knock. Matt, you rush when they open. Sandy, you guard the hallway. I think there are three of them in there. Catch who you can. If your Jesus isn't in there, maybe they can lead us to him."

Pete knocked.

"Who is it?" came a muffled voice from the other side.

"The Virgin Mary," Pete said.

An angry exclamation came through the door. "Are you disrespecting my *mom*?" The door flung open and Pete reached in, grabbed Jesus by the robe, and yanked him into the hallway. I barreled past them into the apartment, where two more Jesuses sat at a table covered in poker chips, empty beer bottles, and cigar butts. One of them wore a black sash over his robe, and the other had the precise look of someone who followed the Law perfectly. Except for the pile of sausage pizza at his elbow.

For a moment, nobody moved. I locked eyes with Legalist Jesus and he stared at me for a long time, saying nothing. He frantically put his cigar out, then pushed the pizza across the table. I kept staring at him and finally he burst, cigar smoke venting from his mouth. "I didn't inhale," he said, and then he jumped to his feet, knocking me backward into the wall. He pushed past Pete and the other Jesus wrestling in the doorway and headed out into the hallway. I heard a crash and anguished cries of "UNCLEAN, UNCLEAN," which I took to mean that Sandy had tackled him.

The last Jesus—the one with the black sash—stood calmly at the table. The window behind him was open, but there was no fire escape. "Looks like you're trapped," I said. But Jesus didn't say anything. He stepped slowly back toward the window.

I took another step toward him. "That's a three-story drop," I said. "You don't want that, do you?"

He glanced over his shoulder, and his eyes darted back to me. In a sudden swirl of cloaks he dove for the window, but

I was right behind him. I grabbed hold of his ankle just as he ascended toward the top of the building. I forgot Jesus could fly. I wedged my legs against the wall and wrapped my fingers into his robe, yanking hard. He still lifted, and my torso moved out of the building. I struggled with my free hand to pull myself back inside, hooking my legs onto the windowsill.

"Hold on," Sandy said, and I could hear her rummaging around in the apartment. A moment later she returned with some rope and told me to wrap it around Jesus' foot. I was losing my grip. After a moment's struggle we got the rope around his ankle, tied it tight, and together yanked him back into the apartment.

I grabbed him by the robe and shook him hard. "You're going to tell me everything you know about Imaginary Jesus!" I shouted.

He scowled at me and said, "Don't count on it."

I shook him again. "What makes you think I won't smash you to bits?"

"My sources say no."

I shoved him into a chair, and Sandy started tying him down. "You know how this is going to end, don't you?"

"Reply hazy, try again."

"That doesn't even make sense."

"You may rely on it," he said. I grabbed his black sash and looked at it more closely. Under a fold of the cloth was a white circle with a black number eight in the center. He was a Magic 8 Ball Jesus.

Pete came in, his shirt torn and chest heaving. "Mine walked through a wall." He pounded the table with his fist. "I chased him outside but he got away."

"Mine got away too," Sandy said. "He bit me!"

Pete sauntered over to our captive Jesus. "Magic 8 Ball Jesus. A lot more common than you would think. People pray to Jesus and then wait to see what answer they'll get. It's interesting. A Magic 8 Ball Jesus only has twenty replies: ten positive, five negative, and five neutral. It's not a great way to plan your life. He's more horoscope than person."

"Ask again later," Jesus said.

"Is he going to be any help?" I asked.

"The only way he'll give us solid answers is by accident." Pete waved him off.

"But we could use him as a hostage," Sandy said.

"I'll barricade the door," I said.

CHAPTER NINE

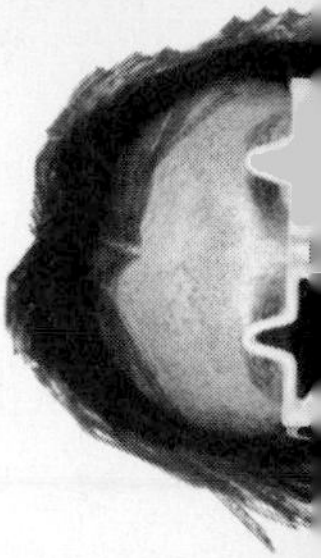

Jesus Will Never Leave You (If You Tie the Knots Tight Enough)

Pete left me and Sandy alone with 8 Ball so he could put the word on the street about our hostage. We played Go Fish for a while. (I can never remember all the rules for poker and Sandy got sick of beating me at it.) Then we entertained ourselves by asking 8 Ball questions.

"Predestination or free will?"

"Concentrate and ask again."

"Should I kill my firstborn son as a sacrifice on a mountain?" Sandy said. She didn't have any kids.

"Outlook not so good."

"If Jesus and some ninjas got in a fight, who would win?"

"Better not tell you now."

That got old pretty quick. I settled back into a broken easy chair and asked Sandy, "What was it like when you first met Jesus?"

Sandy rummaged around in the fridge for a drink, but it was mostly filled with beer. She managed to find one can of soda, and she popped the tab and took a drink. "Surprisingly nice. I thought he would hate me. Here I was, a prostitute, strung out, living with my boyfriend. And we talked about that. Mostly he told me that I didn't have to live my life that way anymore, and that he could help make a way out. And that's what he did."

"Can I ask how you, uh, got into that line of work?"

She looked out the window, like she was looking out into another time. "My boyfriend. He started talking about how much his best friend wanted to sleep with me. He said his friend would give us a hundred bucks and it would be no big deal and we would use the money to go buy me a new dress. He just kept picking at me and picking at me and finally I said okay." She rubbed her knuckles across her eyes. "Afterward, I was crying and he rubbed my back and told me it would be okay, and he took me out and bought me two hundred bucks' worth of clothes." She took a long drink of her soda. "And about a year later I realized he wasn't my boyfriend anymore. He was my pimp. He took care of me, he bought me clothes and food and a place to live and drugs, and I slept with his 'friends' and never saw any money."

She didn't say anything for a long time after that. "I'm sorry," I said.

She shrugged. "The world sucks. What makes me mad are those johns out there, treating women like meat. It's like they don't even realize that every one of those girls grew up somewhere and had hopes and dreams. I grew up in Nashua, Missouri, and I wanted to be a violinist. My dad died when I was seven. I had a dog named Buster. I never had any brothers and sisters, but all the time I was with my boyfriend I kept thinking, *Maybe if I had a brother he would come and take me away from all this.* But no one even thought of me as a person. Even my boyfriend thought of me as cattle."

I didn't say anything, but I felt my face burning. Not because I had ever been a john, but because I knew I had treated that girl from Seattle like meat, like an inconvenience, like an enemy. And there she was, probably just like Sandy, a woman with a story and hopes and dreams but living a nightmare. I didn't try to wake her up. I didn't think of anyone but myself.

"Sandy," I said, "if you ever need anything . . . you're welcome with me and my family."

She smiled and lifted her soda toward me. "Thanks, big brother."

Just then the door exploded inward with a shower of splinters as three huge Jesuses came in through the doorframe. One of them had biceps the size of pumpkins, and his entire body was rippled with veins and muscle. The second had the traditional movie Jesus look but an expression of fierce anger on his face and a whip in one hand. The last had a black leather hat on his head, his long hair pulled into a ponytail. He was wearing a leather vest, leather pants, and a Harley-Davidson shirt pulled tightly over his round belly.

The one with the whip ran into the apartment, grabbed the table, flipped it over, and started swinging his whip all over the place. The bodybuilder flexed his muscles, growled like crazy, yanked some red meat out of the fridge, and started eating it raw. The Harley Jesus crossed his arms and glared at me.

Sandy screamed and ran behind my easy chair, but I jumped up from my seat. "Don't worry," I said. "I went to a Christian school. I recognize these guys."

The one with the whip snarled menacingly at me. Perpetually Angry Jesus. Some people believe that God is always mad at all of humanity because the world is so full of evil. Every once in a while when we do something right we can move into this narrow corner of his not-mad feelings.

"Where's 8 Ball?" he asked through clenched teeth.

"Under the table," I said. "I think you flipped him over when you were breaking the furniture."

"That makes me . . . *mad*!" Perpetually Angry Jesus growled.

The bodybuilder lifted the table and threw it aside. Then he lifted 8 Ball over his head and broke the chair to kindling. The ropes fell off and 8 Ball rubbed his arms. I knew this guy too. Testosterone Jesus, a popular men's retreat speaker. He can tear phone books in half, lie on a bed of nails, or pound an average weakling Christian man into butter.

"You can't kidnap the Lord Almighty," Harley Jesus said. "I'm going to kick you all over creation if you try to keep 8 Ball locked up in here. They don't call me King of the Road for nothing."

I took a gamble, knowing that 8 Ball's responses were completely random. "Magic 8 Ball asked us to tie him up, didn't you, buddy?"

He set his jaw and tried not to say anything. But then Testosterone Jesus shook him and he blurted, "As I see it, yes."

Harley Jesus completely deflated. He's scary looking but means well. "8 Ball, you idiot!" he said. "This is like the time that guy prayed to you and wanted to know if he should write that stupid *Conversations with God* book and you said, 'Yes, definitely.' I swear you cause more trouble. I'm out of here." He tipped his hat to Sandy. "Sorry for the confusion, miss."

"Signs point to yes!" 8 Ball said frantically. But the tide was already shifting in our direction.

I gestured to Testosterone Jesus. "Can I point something

out to you, sir? This woman—" I jerked a thumb at Sandy—"didn't even offer you a meal when you walked in the door."

"Meat. Good," said Testosterone Jesus, holding up the raw meat.

"Yes, but woman no cook! Bad!"

"Grrrrr!" He smashed the table in half.

"What are you doing?" Sandy asked, ducking lower behind the chair.

"She must be punished!" I shouted.

"Raaargh!" He grabbed a plate from the floor, broke it with his teeth, and started moving toward us. As he growled, his massive hands flexed and his teeth gnashed. When he got close enough I put my hand up, palm toward him.

"Are you about to hurt this woman?" I asked in disbelief.

Testosterone Jesus stopped, drool and broken pottery falling from his lips. He struggled to formulate the correct answer. "No?"

"Unbelievable. A man should protect a woman. You are a bad person. You need to go home from this retreat and apologize to your wife."

"Ahuh," Testosterone Jesus said. "Ahuh, ahuh."

"Are you *crying*?" I shook my head. "Jesus wept, but his friend had just *died*. You're crying like a little baby? A little girl baby?"

Testosterone Jesus turned away, his shoulders shaking. I picked up the remote control from the television and put it in his hand. "Go see if football is on," I said gently. "And there's more raw meat in the refrigerator.

"As for you . . ." I turned my attention to Perpetually Angry Jesus. "Here you are, busting up a perfectly fine apartment, and the whole time the Girl Scouts are selling cookies at the Presbyterian church."

"WHAT? HOW DARE THEY TURN MY FATHER'S HOUSE INTO A MARKET?" He stormed out of the room.

8 Ball hung his head in shame. His rescue had been foiled.

Pete came back just after that and looked in wonder at the mess we had made. "I guess the word got out," he said. "Let's put this door back in place."

Moments after we had the door sturdy and locked, someone knocked on it. A strong voice came from outside. "If any man hear my voice, and open the door, I will come in to him."

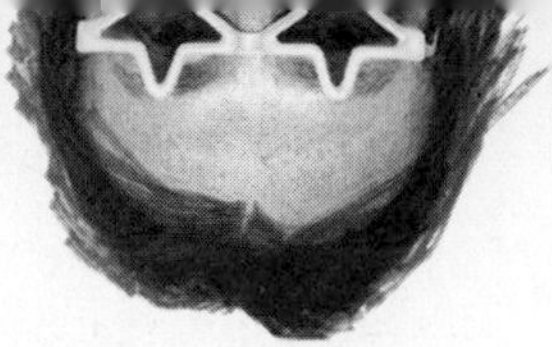

CHAPTER TEN

Behold! I Stand at the Door and Knock!

Testosterone Jesus bellowed from his place on the couch, "WOMAN! GET DOOR!"

Sandy grinned at Pete. "Shall I?"

"Behold!" came the voice from the hallway. "I stand at the door and knock! If any man open the door, I will come in to him."

"I'll get it," I said. "You guys watch 8 Ball." I opened the door, and standing before me was the classical Jesus: honey-colored hair, skin like snow, an almost equine face, blue eyes, white robe, one hand raised as if to knock again.

He swept imperiously past me and his eyes swiftly took in the room. They narrowed when they came across Testosterone Jesus, his feet on the coffee table, raw meat strewn about his mouth and chest.

"Oh, foolish and unwise son," he said. "He is a grief to me, and bitterness to she who bore him."

"What about this guy?" I nodded at 8 Ball. "He can't even say what he wants to."

"Most likely!" 8 Ball said emphatically.

"Every man shall kiss his lips that giveth a right answer," said our new guest.

"That's not much better than 8 Ball," Sandy whispered to me.

"What do you want?" Pete asked.

The new Jesus surveyed the room and finally decided to stand. The damage done by the last group of visitors hadn't left anywhere to sit. "Mine brother is taken captive. Now I beseech thee: let my people go."

"We're not ready to give up our prisoners," I said.

"Then release unto me one prisoner, whomsoever I may desire."

"I don't think so."

Pete whispered in my ear, "Let's talk about this for a minute." He pulled Sandy and me away from King James Jesus and held counsel in the corner of the apartment. "We could let them go and then follow them."

"Won't they just go somewhere else in the complex?"

"I don't think so. I think they're pulling out the stops, sending a lot of heavy hitters to try to get 8 Ball back but still protect Matt's imaginary Jesus."

"Who is 'they'?" I asked.

"Who *are* they?" Sandy corrected.

"The Secret Society of Imaginary Jesuses," Pete said. "An obscure collection of imaginary people who gather to discuss their own importance. Like the Jesus Seminar. Only imaginary."

"Let's trade 8 Ball for Imaginary Jesus," I suggested.

"I don't think he'll go for it. King James Jesus drives a hard bargain. It was centuries before he even allowed New King James Jesus to exist." Pete pulled his big fingers restlessly through his beard.

"We should at least try," I said. Pete nodded his agreement. I stood and approached King James Jesus. "We'll make an exchange. 8 Ball for my imaginary Jesus."

King James Jesus' face twisted into a superior, knowing smile. "I am wont to release unto thee a prisoner," he said. "But methinks thy choice shall be a hard judgment, transgressors." He pulled a manila envelope from his robe and tossed it to me. "Behold!"

I grabbed it and pulled out a glossy black-and-white photograph. It was a picture of a donkey with a white star on her nose. Around her neck was fastened today's paper, the date clearly visible.

King James Jesus laughed heartily and cried out, "Thine ass is mine!"

CHAPTER ELEVEN

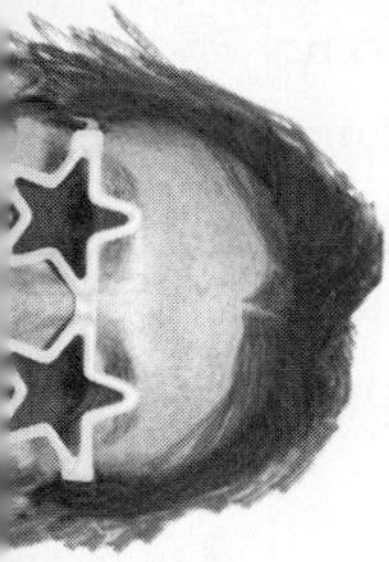

!!!!!

Before we go on, I have a couple of comments. One, *good grief, they kidnapped Daisy!* That is upsetting. Two, I know some of you men who love men's retreats are angry about some comments in recent chapters, and I want to say that men's retreats are fine and dandy. So please stop sitting in front of your wife's computer trying to peck out the letters to send an angry e-mail. Three, you may have noticed that King James Jesus said *ass*, and I would like to apologize on his behalf. His translation is four hundred years old now. When he says *ass*, he really means *donkey*. He had no idea that his comment "Thine ass is mine" would sound either offensive or funny. In fact, he looked at me in complete consternation when I broke into a fit of hysterical laughter.

Please don't send me letters saying, "Jesus (even an imaginary Jesus) would never use offensive words of any kind." Maybe you have forgotten the story where Jesus was walking with his brother James to the synagogue and they were about to cross the street and Jesus grabbed James and said, "Look out for that dog poop."

Yes, he said *poop*. I mean, you can't get through life without saying it sometimes. So you can look up that story—it's somewhere or other, maybe in the Apocrypha. Or maybe Imaginary Jesus told me that story. I would like to point out, though, that neither James nor Jesus ever saw the dog that left that little surprise package right in the middle of the road. I shake my fist at you, Houdini Dog! Is nowhere safe from you?

Now I can't remember what we were talking about.

Oh yeah. *Good grief, they kidnapped Daisy!*

We looked closely at the picture, and we recognized her immediately. Sandy couldn't figure out why we were so upset about a donkey being held captive, except that she lived in Portland and thus believed that all animals should be free. So when she looked at King James Jesus and said, "You monsters!" she mostly just meant, *Boy is it ever mean to keep an animal all tied up*. I pointed out that we had 8 Ball tied up, and she pointed out that 8 Ball was, after all, imaginary and this appeared to be a real, flesh-and-bone donkey, and then I pointed out that "flesh-and-bone" was a weird way to refer to a donkey, what with all the fur, and maybe we should say "fur-and-bone" and then Sandy got mad and I suddenly realized that I was really getting along with Sandy and treating her like a sister.

We had a short conference and made a plan. I would go with King James Jesus and 8 Ball to make the switch. We would allow Testosterone Jesus to go along, because KJJ probably didn't realize that I had him completely under my control. That would give me an advantage. Also, wherever we went I would be able to keep an eye out for Imaginary Jesus, because I knew what he looked like. Pete had seen him only once, and Sandy hadn't seen him at all.

I told KJJ that I would be coming with him, and that we would give them Testosterone Jesus and 8 Ball in exchange for Daisy. Then Testosterone Jesus started blubbering like a baby and saying, "I stay with pretty lady!" and I had to start quoting lines from *Braveheart* to calm him down.

"This shall propitiate me and cause me to become consistent in my actions toward thee."

I ignored KJJ and said good-bye to Pete. "I think we're really going to pull this off."

He smiled, but not with his eyes, and put his hand on my shoulder. "Once we get ahold of Imaginary Jesus, this whole thing will be almost behind us." He cocked his head and gave me a quizzical look, but he didn't say anything more.

I asked, "That's what we're doing, right?" But he didn't answer.

I gave Sandy a hug and told her that she was my favorite ex-prostitute with a heart of gold, and she punched me in the stomach and said that she didn't like me at all. That reminded me of the Frog of Hate, and I reached into my pocket and was pleased to find him still there, eight chapters later.

I walked out onto the street, close behind KJJ and 8 Ball. Their heads were close together in what appeared to be an intense conversation, though I couldn't conceive of any coherent conversation they could possibly have.

I patted Testosterone Jesus on the shoulder and told him that soon he would be free to do as he pleased. He joyfully lifted his arms in the air and shouted, *"Freeeeeeeeeeeeeeeeeeeeedoooooooooom!"*

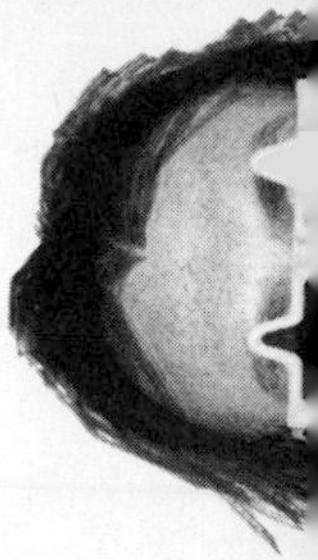

CHAPTER TWELVE

The Secret Society of Imaginary Jesuses

Thirteen blocks from the squalid apartment where we captured 8 Ball, the headquarters of the Secret Society of Imaginary Jesuses occupied an entire high-rise in the downtown area, just on the edge of the Pearl. A simple logo with the letters *SSIJ* adorned the front door, and we walked into a large foyer with dark, angular surfaces that shone in the reflected light. A stern-looking Jesus in a judge's robe sat behind the counter just in front of the bank of elevators.

He stood as we entered. KJJ growled when he saw the Jesus behind the counter. "Behold!" quoth he. "I have brought forth the captive 8 Ball, and lo, the most virile of the imaginary Jesuses is with me, and the man called Matt Mikalatos. Now make way for our ascent."

"And what will you give me in exchange?" asked the Jesus in the robes. I studied him carefully and realized that I knew him. In fact, I had done business with him before. He was Bargain Jesus, the Jesus who would always answer your prayers . . . for a price.

"Fie on thee!" KJJ cried. "Not one more bargain shall be struck between me and thee."

A deep frown creased Bargain Jesus' face. "Then you cannot use my elevator."

"Let's take the stairs," I said.

"The stairs are mine as well," he said. "To ascend will require a sacrifice. Promise that you will read your Bible every day for the rest of your life, and that you will never again miss church, and that you will tell every stranger you meet on an airplane about me, and in exchange I will allow you to use the elevator."

"Thou rascal," KJJ said, with dark foreboding in his voice. "I shall summon Perpetually Wroth Jesus to tan thy hinder parts."

"I go church!" Testosterone Jesus shouted, and he clapped his hands gleefully.

I leaned against the counter and looked at 8 Ball. "Will you tell every stranger you meet on an airplane about Bargain Jesus?"

"It is certain," he answered, a look of panic on his face.

I rolled my eyes and turned to KJJ. "You already read the Bible every day. You practically worship it."

"Verily, thou speakest truth," he admitted grudgingly.

Bargain Jesus bowed and gestured toward the elevators. We went over and pressed the button. Nearby I could see a Jesus with a gray uniform and no mouth sweeping the floor.

"That's Liberal Social Services Jesus," Bargain Jesus said. "He thinks the best way to tell people about God is through service, but he never talks about God. He's great to have around because he keeps the place spotless."

"That does sound nice," I said. "I should invite him over to my house sometime when Krista isn't home. She'd love to come home to a spotless house."

"Sometimes his brother, Conservative Truth-Telling Jesus comes around. He has no arms. He thinks the only way to tell people about God is through hard truth, and he never raises a hand to help people with their physical needs. He's difficult to handle, honestly."

Ding! The elevator had arrived. We stepped on and the doors shut. KJJ hit the button for the seventh floor, and as the elevator rose, Testosterone Jesus slapped himself in the forehead. "Today Sunday?" he asked.

"No," I said.

"I miss church?" He started crying.

I put my hand on his shoulder. "You didn't miss church." When you make as many rash, fragile vows as Testosterone Jesus, it can make for a tortured and guilt-ridden experience.

The door opened to an expansive office that filled the entire floor. We stepped out, and over by one of the windows I saw a man wearing a suit, his back turned toward us. Beside him stood a donkey, also looking down over the city of Portland, with its bridges and network of streets, and in the distance Mount Hood rising up, clouds surrounding her like anxious servants.

The man turned and smiled. He had short hair, sparkling eyes, perfect teeth, and no beard, but I could tell he was a Jesus of some sort. His suit was clearly expensive, and his tie was perfectly knotted. He motioned to Daisy. "Here's your donkey, Matt. I'm sorry for the confusion."

I pushed 8 Ball toward him. "Here's your made-up Jesus," I said. "Who are you?"

"He's one of the more popular imaginary Jesuses," Daisy answered.

"He doesn't have a beard," I said.

The Suit smiled. "Studies show that most Americans find clean-shaven people to be more honest and trustworthy than people with beards." He nodded to 8 Ball, Testosterone, and KJJ. "If you gentlemen will excuse us, I'd like a few moments alone with Mr. Mikalatos and his donkey friend." 8 Ball left without a word, and KJJ gave me a brief, businesslike handshake. Testosterone Jesus punched me in the arm and slapped me on the rear.

"I hear you have a parking ticket," the beardless Jesus said. "May I see it?"

I pulled the crumpled pink slip out of my pocket.

"This was a major failing on the part of your imaginary Jesus, was it?"

"Yeah, I got suspicious when my omnipotent best friend couldn't keep me from getting a parking ticket."

Jesus straightened the paper out on his desk. "Some Jesuses are more convincing than others. People invent a Jesus for one specific reason and then discard him when they don't need him anymore. A good example would be You-Should-Get-a-Divorce-and-Marry-a-Younger-Woman Jesus. To be honest, he barely meets the requirements of being an imaginary Jesus, and we've suggested that he join our sister organization as a Pure Reckless Fantasy Jesus."

"I think we should be on our way." Daisy edged toward the door.

"Wait," I said. "Let's hear him out."

"Thank you, Matt. I knew you would be reasonable. The point is, some imaginary Jesuses are better than others. Your Jesus was a relatively sophisticated one. The fact is, however, you're ready to trade him in for a better one."

"A much better one," Daisy said. "Like maybe the real one."

Jesus laughed. He clapped me on the shoulder, and we stared out the window together. "Let's be frank, Matt. The real Jesus is inconvenient. He doesn't always show up when you call. He asks for unreasonable things. He frightens people. He can be immensely frustrating. But you can still serve him while working with an imaginary Jesus. We provide a service to get people closer to God." He picked up the phone on his desk and pressed a button. "Jesus here. I'd like you to fix a parking ticket for me. Matt Mikalatos. Yes. Thank you." He handed me the slip of paper. "I took care of this for you."

"Who *are* you?"

"I'm Political Power Jesus," he said. "And together we can accomplish amazing things. If you follow me we, could eradicate abortion. We could promote family values via legislation. We could make sure that kids can learn about Creation at school, and that they can pray whenever they please—a basic human right. We could implement green policies. We could eliminate poverty by pumping more money into welfare. We could bring justice to the world and show people what it looks like to serve God. We could be an example to the nations." He paused. "And of course, there's money to be had as well. I bought this building, this suit, my home, my BMW, all while serving God in this way."

"Matt," Daisy said.

"Quiet, I'm thinking."

Political Jesus leaned close. "If you come to me, Matt, you can have power and much more. But you will have to be completely committed to me. There won't be room for other ideas about Jesus or for questioning me."

A sudden voice bellowed an echoing cry from behind us.

"GET AWAY FROM HIM!" We turned to see a Jesus running toward us, his robe and powder blue sash flapping like a flag. "He belongs to me!"

A familiar feeling of fondness washed over me. It was Imaginary Jesus, the one I had invented, my Jesus of choice, and I was glad to see him.

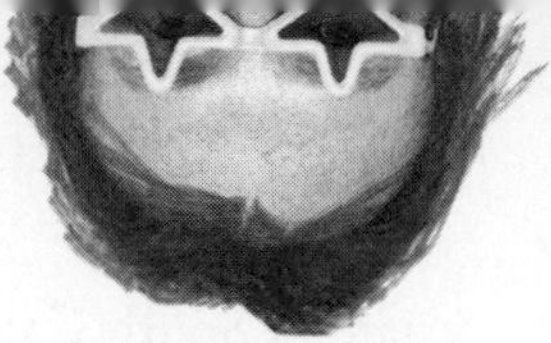

CHAPTER THIRTEEN

Thy Kingdom Come

Imaginary Jesus and I had an awkward moment when we tried to figure out if we should hug or not and finally settled on the handshake-that-turns-into-a-hug. Daisy sighed loudly.

"I'm glad you're here," said Political Jesus. "Now Matt can see my superiority firsthand."

"Matt created me. I'm his ideal Christ. I always agree with him, I don't enforce unpleasant rules, and I never tell him that he eats too much. How will you compete with that?"

Political Jesus grinned, and his canine teeth were sharp and gleaming. "I'm so glad you asked. I've brought a guest so that he can share what it's like to follow me." He gestured to a far wall and when it opened, a man came out wearing what appeared to be clothes from *Little House on the Prairie*.

"Pa Ingalls?" I asked.

"I'm a follower of a political Jesus," he said. "Specifically, of Christian Nation Jesus. My name is Jeffrey Jones, and I'm a leader in one of his movements in South Carolina."

"Oh no," Daisy said.

Jeffrey turned on a display screen, and a picture of the

state of South Carolina came up with a bloodred cross in the center, rays of white light radiating out to the edges. "In 2003, Political Jesus encouraged some of us to come up with a solution to the moral degradation of American culture. Corruption was rotting the halls of power like furry mold on a wheel of cheese."

I smacked my forehead. "And what brilliant plan did you come up with? Guerrilla warfare?"

Political Jesus frowned. "Please allow my associate to continue."

Jeffrey pointed to the screen, and the logo was replaced by a station wagon packed full of luggage and children, a smiling and wholesome-looking Midwestern couple waving from in front of the car. "Our goal was to move thousands of Christians into South Carolina and take over the government by becoming the majority voting bloc."

I started laughing like crazy. "You're kidding," I said when I could get a breath. "Ha-ha-ha-hahaaaa!"

"I am not kidding."

"What would you do if you managed to take control?" Daisy said.

"Secede from the United States and become the first truly Christian nation."

"And the national song would be 'Kumbaya,'" I said, getting into the spirit of things.

Jeffrey stood very straight and still. "Our new nation will remain long after this morally decrepit exemplar of slavery and godlessness has been laid to waste."

"And you'll have to be a Christian to vote, I suppose, and the only music will be hymns, and all the bookstores will be

Christian bookstores, and if you want to buy pornography, why, there will only be Christian porn," I said.

"There won't be pornography in our nation," he said.

"Sure, and no one will yell at their spouses, and children will be unfailingly obedient, and the lion will lie down with the lamb."

"This will be a home-centered economy," he said, his voice rising. "We'll have intentional community—"

"Potlucks," Daisy said.

"—house churches—"

"That's all the rage in Portland," I said.

"—unlicensed homeschooling with no testing criteria—"

"It's not the government's business if we have ignorant kids," I said.

"—unlicensed ministry—"

"That should help the cults spread faster," Daisy said cheerfully.

"—and home gardening!"

We didn't have anything to say to that one.

Jeffrey pounded the table. "We will live brave and godly lives that don't require prostrating ourselves to the imperial magistrate!"

I cleared my throat carefully. "I don't want to upset you, but isn't the whole point of this that you'll *be* the imperial magistrate?"

Political Jesus excused Jeffrey, who stalked out, trying to contain his anger. "That did not go as I had hoped," said Political Jesus.

"That's the danger of following an imaginary Jesus," Daisy said. "The more committed you get to him and his plan, the further afield from the real Jesus you get. Your earnest attempts to be committed to your imaginary Jesus actually move you away from Christ."

I sighed. "I like a lot of what you're saying, Political Jesus. And you know that in the past I've followed you, at least briefly. But Jesus' most political statement in the Bible was, 'Pay your taxes.'"

Daisy nodded. "It's not like the Roman occupationist government was a godly, loving government, either. They had slavery. They used crucifixion as a punishment for thieves, runaway slaves, and political dissidents."

"They wore skirts," I said.

"They had a terrible history regarding animal rights," Daisy added.

"Still," I said, "Jesus didn't gather a crowd, stand up, and say, 'Hey! Everybody pack your bags! We're moving to Joppa, taking over the city council, and kicking out the Romans!' Hoooraaaaay! Shouts of acclaim from the crowd! Much rejoicing!"

"God cares about politics," Political Jesus said.

"He does," Daisy said. "Because at the end of the day politics is about people. Soon he will rule over every government as King of kings. But right now he seems most concerned about whether a nation is just and righteous and whether they take care of the poor and widows."

Jeffrey burst into the room and hurried over to us. "I was so flustered during my presentation that I forgot a major point. We would do away with the laws that force emergency rooms to treat people with no insurance."

I stared at him in stunned silence. I tried to control my

anger, but I could feel a scowl growing on my face. I told myself, *He means well. He's really trying to do the right thing.* But I didn't believe it. "So you'll have waiting rooms full of impoverished dead people," I said evenly.

"No, that's not the point, I—"

"If you ever manage to take over South Carolina," I said, "I would rather live in the first century. They may not have bathrooms or air fresheners, but at least they don't stink. Get out of my sight."

Jeffrey hung his head and slowly walked away.

Political Jesus rubbed his chin thoughtfully. "An unfortunate example. I should have brought in a senator or president, so you could see the beauty of serving God and having power in the government. I wish you could see the glory that was Rome, or what it was like when Constantine ruled Byzantium."

A gruff voice called from the back of the room. "It's all about power with you, man. What about love?"

CHAPTER FOURTEEN

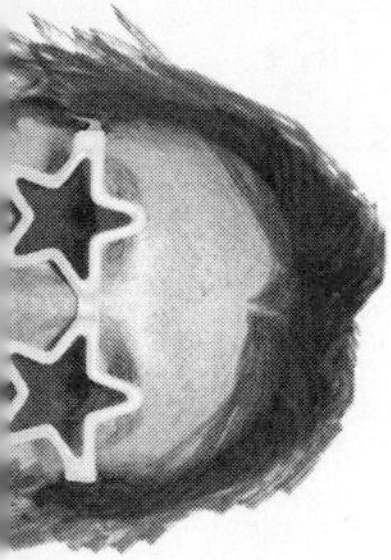

Onward Christian Soldiers

Daisy and I turned and saw a lean, robed Jesus with flowers plaited into his hair.

Political Jesus made a disgusted face. "Is that you, Hippie Jesus?"

"I prefer Peacenik Jesus. And your military might didn't do you much good in Constantinople when the Muslims came, kicked you out, and turned it into Istanbul."

"The sword is a necessary tool in politics," Political Jesus said, his face turning red. "At least I'm not a coward."

"Leading a protest without any weapons takes more bravery than you'll ever have!" And before we could do anything, Peacenik Jesus leaped for Political Jesus, grabbed him around the shoulders, and bit his ear.

With an animal roar, Political Jesus pushed him off, knocking him into the table.

Peacenik felt his robes and stuck his hand inside. "You broke my iPhone!" He leveled a kick straight into Political Jesus' shin. "Stick it to the Man!"

Imaginary Jesus, Daisy, and I stepped to the side. A

paperweight zipped by, bounced off the window, and left a ding in it. Political Jesus jumped on top of his desk and took a flying leap at Peacenik, and they tumbled to the floor. Peacenik gave Political a couple of quick punches to the kidney, then propped him standing up, took a running start, and clothes-lined him. Political Jesus rolled over and scissored Peacenik's feet out from under him.

"You know," my Jesus said, "legislating behavior doesn't change people's hearts. Those two are talking about bringing peace to the world and they can't even get along with each other."

"I think you are a better Jesus than both of them," I said.

"Thanks."

"Still not the *real* Jesus," Daisy said. "Societal transformation can only come through personal revolution. Which only comes from the Holy Spirit. End of story."

"Right," I said. "Oooh!" Peacenik had crashed a vase full of water over Political Jesus' head. "We should find a way to stop all this."

Just then Political Jesus took a swing at Peacenik with a heavy metal bar, missing him but smashing me right in the face.

The last thing I heard was Political Jesus shouting, "Quick! Go get Televangelist Jesus!"

CHAPTER FIFTEEN

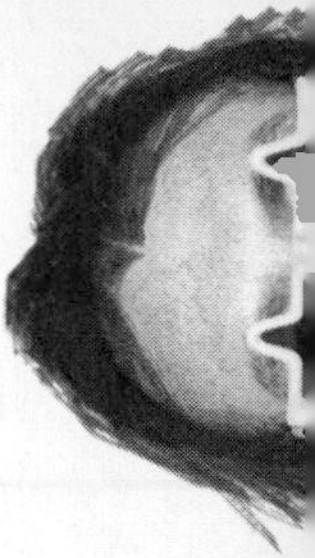

Boy Meets Bunny

The first thing I saw when I came through my heavy-metal-bar-to-the-face-induced haze was another beardless Jesus, this one looking a lot like Steve Martin, complete with white suit and bunny ears.

"What's with the bunny ears?" I asked groggily.

"The Law-duh Almightee told me, 'I want you to listen to me like a creature with big ears,' and I said, 'What creature has bigger ears than a bunny?' And he said nothing. And so I am wearing these ears for the next thirty-two days."

"Oh," I said. "Elephants have big ears too."

"I can heal you," he said.

"It's just a headache."

"But you must have . . . *faith!*"

"I have faith."

"Also . . . twenty dollars."

"Twenty? I can buy aspirin for five. In fact, Imaginary Jesus has some."

TV Jesus threw his arms out to the side. "Fine. You have the faith but not the cash so let me say—sum booya soya—I will do this one for free and HACHA!" and he blew on me. He hit me right in the middle of my forehead with his palm and I fell backward.

And my headache went away. I sat up and felt my forehead. "Are you kidding me? That actually worked?"

TV Jesus started laughing like crazy. He started jumping up and down. He held out his hand for a high five from Peacenik Jesus and received his five. He pointed at Political Jesus with two fingers and then gave him two thumbs up.

He helped me up, saying, "If you follow me, you will have the life you always wanted. Money! Wealth! Big house! Fancy plane! Unending health!"

"Chicks?" Peacenik Jesus asked.

TV Jesus considered this. "Hmmm. Okay. Just don't tell anyone!"

"Yay!" said Peacenik Jesus.

"What does unending health mean?" I asked.

"Never . . . sick . . . again! *Hallelujah!*"

I frowned. "Never sick again. So your followers . . . never die?"

TV Jesus spun in a circle and his hands exploded outward. "Not if they have . . . *faith!*"

"So you're saying that if I have faith, I'll never be sick. You're saying that if I have faith, nothing bad will ever happen to me?"

"Matt," Daisy said, "You don't want to follow this—"

"GET OUT!" I took a swing at TV Jesus.

He leaped backward and spread his hands wide. "I can see you've had pain in your life," he said. "Moments of doubt that have introduced themselves into your life as sickness, financial ruin, trouble in relationships!"

"Where's that heavy metal bar?" I asked.

"You can't hurt me," TV Jesus said. "The *joy* of the *Law-duh* is my strength!" Imaginary Jesus came up to me and put his arm around my shoulder. "I know that must be hard to hear."

"You're no better than him." I shrugged off his arm and headed for the exit.

"Happy feet!" TV Jesus shouted. "I have happy feet. Sorry about this, it just happens sometimes." And he started to dance around the room.

"C'mon, Daisy," I said. "Let's get out of here." We went out the door, Imaginary Jesus behind us.

"I'm coming too," he said.

"Okay," I said. "But none of these others. I have to get away from them."

"Bounce! Bounce! Bounce!" TV Jesus shouted. "I'm not a *jack*rabbit, I'm a *Jesus* rabbit!"

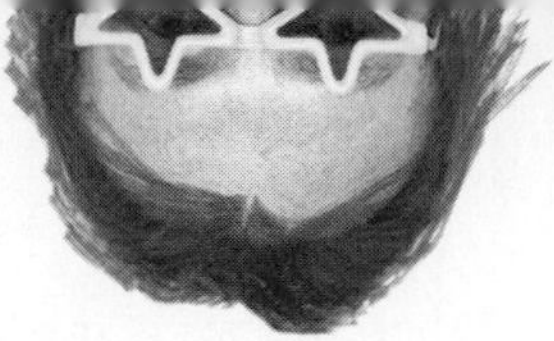

CHAPTER SIXTEEN

Healing in the Bedroom

My wife likes pitch-black darkness at night. The sort of dark where the tiny LED of a cell phone charging makes you squint. The kind of dark that makes the smoke alarm look like a helicopter with a spotlight. Darkness of this magnitude causes otherwise ordinary human beings to walk like mummies. First you put your arms straight out in front of you. Then you shuffle your feet so that you don't kick anything. Then you make moaning sounds. Usually this is because you forgot to shuffle your feet and you kicked something hard. You're not sure what, because it is too dark to see your feet.

One night, lying in our familiar darkness, talking about our day, Krista started crying. She was crying because I was leaving for a business trip in a few short hours. I had a 6 a.m. flight to catch, which meant leaving the house at around four. Krista would be alone with the kids for the week, and her wrists had become increasingly painful over the last several months. We thought maybe it was carpal tunnel syndrome. In recent weeks she hadn't even been able to type on the computer. I had tried to convince her to go to the doctor, but she hadn't had time. So here we were, me leaving on a trip, and Krista facing the prospect of being stuck at home and in pain. There was nothing to be done but for her to have a lousy week and hope she could get some prescription drugs sometime soon.

So I held her hands and prayed for her. Some people say prayer is "just talking to God," but I think that's a dumb way to say it. There are enormous numbers of people who approach their gods on their stomachs, begging for a moment's attention. We, on the other hand, walk up to him like we're walking up to the guy at the counter of 7-Eleven: "Hey, I'd like two of those packs of cigarettes and a slushy." *Excuse me,* someone asks, *what are you doing there?* "Oh, just talking to the 7-Eleven guy." The fact that he allows us this friendly accessibility astounds me.

Anyway, I asked God to comfort Krista during my absence. I prayed that the kids wouldn't behave in a way that would bring on bouts of insanity for anyone around them. Then I prayed that Jesus would heal her hands. I focused all my attention on this request. I wanted to make it clear that this would mean a lot to us, that we would love to see her hands healed. Krista thanked me for praying and we talked for a while longer.

A few minutes later she lifted her hands in the air, twisted her wrists around, and said, "That's weird." I could see her hands, a darker shadow in a room full of darkness, and I could see them turning, twisting around like wind chimes. She was flexing her fingers and rotating her wrists.

"What?" I asked.

"The pain in my wrists just . . . stopped."

I thought about that for a minute. "Do they stop hurting sometimes?"

"No, the pain has been constant. But now it's gone."

"That's amazing." I stared at the ceiling. Or rather, I stared in the direction of the ceiling—I couldn't see it in the dark. What had just happened? I didn't feel comfortable with the obvious answer. After we had lain in silence for a few minutes I asked her, "Do you think Jesus just healed your hands?"

Krista rotated her wrists. "The pain will probably come back tomorrow." But it didn't. I called her from my business trip. She said maybe when the business trip was over the pain would come back. Maybe this was a little gift to help her through the week. But it didn't come back after that trip. It didn't ever come back.

As strange as this may sound, this obvious answer to our prayer frightened me. This was an unexpected and slightly terrifying Jesus. I had been told at various Christian outlets, by people who should know, that Jesus doesn't wander around healing people anymore. In the first century, maybe, but not the twenty-first. Also, they had said, Jesus wouldn't do it in the "Christianized" world. He would do it in some little tribal group that had never heard of him, deep in some jungle where scientists and doctors feared to tread, as a way of proving his divinity.

And yet, here we were, the recipients of what appeared to be a genuine healing. We prayed and the damage to Krista's hands went away. Right there in our bedroom in Vancouver, Washington. We were not unbelievers who needed a miraculous sign of the power of God. We weren't tribal people who had never heard of Jesus. We were twenty-first-century Americans, Christians from the majority ethnic group of our nation. We didn't show much evidence of faith, and yet there he was, making the sick well in answer to prayer.

How do you deal with a God who breaks all the rules that

your confident, well-meaning friends have told you he will follow? They had told me that he wouldn't invade my life with inconveniences like miracles, things that make me stop and realize the fragile, illusory nature of nature. And here he was, showing me that little things like pain and death and the rules of the universe weren't going to get in the way of his doing whatever he liked. I can remember lying there in the dark and thinking, *If this is true, then he can do whatever he pleases. Who knows what he might ask of me? I can't control him. I can't box him in with my own beliefs and philosophies.*

Pete, Sandy, and Daisy listened in silence as I explained all this to them. We had found one of Portland's ubiquitous coffee shops near the SSIJ headquarters. Imaginary Jesus stood off to the side, his arms crossed. He had not received a warm welcome from Pete or Sandy. Daisy ignored him completely and had, in fact, trodden on his sandaled foot with her hoof, studiously ignoring his yowls of pain.

Pete shook his great bearded head and said, "Matt, the way you're saying all this, it almost sounds like an accusation. Are you angry at God for healing Krista?"

"No." My protest didn't sound convincing, even to me.

"There's something you're not sharing," Sandy said. "Something painful."

"It's not a big deal," I said. "People have had worse. A lot worse."

Pete drummed his fingers on the table for a long time, staring at Daisy. "You need to talk about this. I suspect that this pain leads to the heart of your imaginary Jesus problems."

"I've talked about it with Krista. I've dealt with this."

Pete jerked his thumb at Jesus, who was leaning against the

wall and picking at the wounds in his palm. "Why is *he* still here, then?"

I shrugged. "He's close enough to the real thing, I guess."

Pete stood up and walked to the door. His face was red and he was clenching his hands. "I need some fresh air," he said, and he flung the door open.

"We should probably go too," Sandy said. "Let's walk back over to my place and we can talk about this some more."

I didn't say anything, but I followed Sandy and Daisy out the door. Imaginary Jesus tagged along behind. It was raining, and the yellow glow of the streetlights revealed the slanting rain in white relief against the darkness. Portlanders had pulled their hoods up and walked about their business as always, not rushing, not leaping under awnings, just living with it, the fact and reality of precipitation.

As we walked across the street, a motorcycle revved its engine and came barreling toward us. That one headlight, like an eye, locked on me and came at me, fast. I froze for a moment and a million thoughts went through my head. Had I done something to anger a motorcycle gang? Not that I recalled. Was it possible that I had an identical twin brother who had angered a motorcycle gang? This seemed plausible, but I had no way to know if it might be true. As the motorcycle came nearer I could tell it was a Red Wing, white and red with flames and eyes along the side. The rider hit the brakes and slid sideways up beside me. He yanked off his helmet, and a familiar face with blue, smiling eyes and a curly mop of blond hair greeted me.

"Dude," he said. "I hear you need some help."

"Motorcycle Guy?" I asked. "Is that you?"

CHAPTER SEVENTEEN

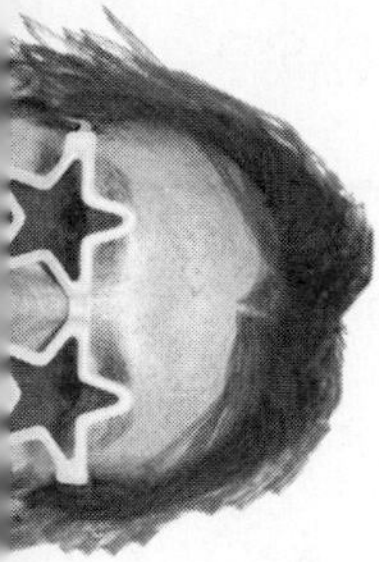

Every Cowboy Sings a Sad, Sad Song

I first met Motorcycle Guy because of Sarah. She and I had dated for a year and a half before she went away on an exchange program to Germany. In those ancient days, one did not use free Internet phones to call loved ones overseas. No! Instead, one worked hard for money, scrounged for it in the sofa cushions, sold recyclables, delivered newspapers, and so on, and then handed one crisp dollar to the phone company for every minute spent hurling one's voice across the Atlantic. It was the 1990s.

I called Sarah for her birthday. We talked for about forty dollars. I don't remember much about the call, other than the fact that the end of our conversation went like this:

"Good-bye, Sarah. I love you."

Pause.

"Did you get my letter yet?" Sarah asked.

"You sent me a letter? That's great! No, I haven't gotten it yet."

"I love you too," she said. "Bye."

The next day I skipped out to the mailbox, *tra la la*, and what do you think I found there? Yes! A letter from my girlfriend! Hooray! I tore it open, the tissue-paper airmail letter giving way to my fumbling fingers.

"Dear Matt," it started. It would be best if we stopped seeing each other. She would no longer be my girlfriend. She would be free to laugh raucously with her friends in Germany. And so on.

Although Sarah and I had dated only a year and a half or so, in my mind I had constructed a future reality in which we got married and brought forth several healthy, well-behaved children. We grew old together and she still looked like a high schooler but with slightly gray hair, and then we died together, lying in bed and smiling serenely, because we knew we would spend more time together frolicking in clouds and playing harps.

I took to wandering the streets around my neighborhood, weeping. Full-bodied, moaning, chest-racking sobs of grief. Well-meaning neighbors peered over their backyard fences to ask if I needed something. Thieves hid under their beds thinking my wails were police sirens. Irish neighbors closed their shades, thinking a banshee had come for their children. Neighborhood animals congregated and followed me from a respectful distance. I prayed as I cried, to make sure that God knew about my suffering, just in case he wanted to intervene.

One evening, as I made my midnight tour of the neighborhood, I realized that I needed something more than a teenage sob-fest. I needed . . . music.

I cried out, "God, I need to learn how to play guitar so I can write songs that will show . . . you . . . my . . . *pain*!"

As these words left my lips I saw a guitar, propped up against a garbage can. Someone had discarded it in the precise place where I happened to pray for a guitar. Amazed by God's goodness, I picked it up and strummed it as I walked along.

The guitar was horribly out of tune. Having never held a guitar before, I didn't know how to tune it, but my ears assured me all was not right. Now I walked the neighborhood weeping, praying, and strumming an out-of-tune guitar. But even this pitiful picture did not satisfy me, and I decided that the depressed vibe from a sad place would fit my mood better.

A kid my age had wrapped his car around a fence post and died earlier in the week, and the sidewalk near there was festooned with flowers and cards, photos and washed-out chalk messages on the sidewalk. I decided that this place would be sad enough, so I sat down on the curb, strummed my guitar, and felt sorry for myself.

I hadn't been there long before a man on a motorcycle came tearing down the road. As he approached me he slowed, then pulled over. A woman was riding behind him, clutching his back. He pulled off his helmet and said, "Dude." (I grew up in California.) "Did you know that guy?"

I tore myself from the reverie of my own relentless pain and looked around, trying to think who Motorcycle Guy was talking about. "What guy?" I asked him.

"The dead guy." He gestured to the flowers. The candles. The cards. His girlfriend had taken off her helmet now too, and she was beautiful in the way that someone else's girlfriend is beautiful when your own girlfriend has crushed your heart so she can be free in Germany. I could tell she felt sorry for me and my supposed dead friend.

"Oh," I said. "No. My girlfriend just broke up with me."

Motorcycle Guy and his beautiful girlfriend exchanged a

sad but knowing glance. Then he held out his hand. "Give me that guitar." He put his kickstand down and sat back on the motorcycle, expertly tuning the guitar. "I'm going to sing you a song." And he proceeded to do just that. I listened in mute wonder as he sang every verse, every chorus, every bridge and refrain of the song "Every Rose Has Its Thorn." You know the words, I'm sure. Roses have thorns, nights have dawns, and cowboys sing sad songs. Love hurts.

"That song is really true," he said. Then he handed me the guitar. "This guitar's neck is warped; it'll never hold a tune. It ought to be in the garbage." Then he and his girlfriend got back on his bike. They waved to me and rocketed away. *Doing a wheelie.*

I sat there in stunned, slack-jawed amazement. I looked around for the camera crew, certain that somehow I had wandered into a John Cusack movie. I tried, experimentally, to cry again. But every time a tear welled up, I would think of Motorcycle Guy and I would laugh. Every time I cried about Sarah after that, it ended with me thinking, *Hey, be careful or some guy will come up on at least one wheel of a motorcycle, grab your guitar, and sing a rock ballad.* I never got a chance to thank him or his beautiful girlfriend. Sometimes I wished I would see him again so I could say, "Thanks, Motorcycle Guy. You got me through a rough patch." Then I would get all quiet and say, awkwardly, "Is it possible that you and your girlfriend are some sort of angels? Because coincidences like this one are uncommon and have the flavor of something planned, like maybe God sent you."

Or maybe I would just say thanks. I never planned it out sufficiently because I didn't think I would ever see him again.

But here he was, in the middle of the street in Portland, the rain coming down and getting in his hair and all over his motorcycle, and I was standing in the middle of the street, trying to think of something to say.

"How's your girlfriend?" I asked.

"Come on," he said. "I want to show you something."

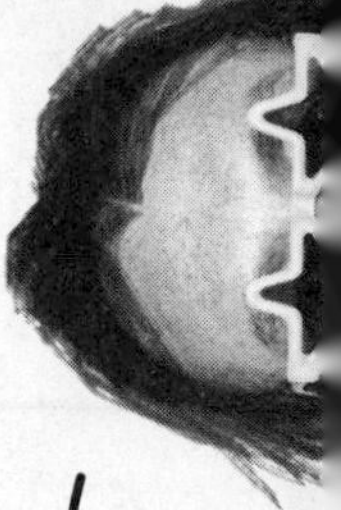

CHAPTER EIGHTEEN

A Funny Thing Happened on the Way to the Emergency Room

Motorcycle Guy took Burnside to the 405. We crossed the bridge and headed north on I-5. I asked him where we were going, but either he didn't hear me or he was ignoring me. The temperature dropped for a moment as we crossed the Columbia, and Motorcycle Guy hit the gas to speed past the laboring semis. We passed the exit to my place. I tapped him on the helmet, but he leaned forward and hit the gas again. He finally exited at 134th, then headed up Highway 99, turning in at the entry to Legacy Salmon Creek Hospital.

He pulled into the emergency room parking lot. I got off the motorcycle and he did the same, pulling off his helmet and hanging it on the handlebars.

"You know someone here?" I asked.

"No," he said. "But I know you were here a few months ago. I thought you might give me the guided tour."

"But I don't have a tour guide license," I said.

"You're always hiding behind something funny. Let's talk about your real life for once."

I racked my brain trying to think of something funny about

the emergency room. And do you know what's funny about the hospital? Nothing. There have been sitcoms and comedies about hospitals, of course, but the humor comes from the characters and situations, not from the hospital itself. The only consistent joke is about those little gowns that don't cover your rear, but even that isn't funny, really. It's a strike against human dignity.

This is the closest I have to a funny hospital story: This one time at my church in California, just after I had graduated college, there was this semipro wrestler named American Eagle who had become a Christian. He wore this big red, white, and blue shirt and blue warm-up pants. One Sunday, as an outreach to the community around us, we put up a portable wrestling ring, and some of American Eagle's friends came to put on a big exposition for us. Afterward, a bunch of us volunteered to help take the ring down and get it all packed up.

At one point I was helping pick up some of the ropes from the side of the ring, and someone else was unscrewing something from one of the large metal posts at the corners. Then someone shouted, "LOOK OUT!" and in slow motion that giant, heavy pole came speeding toward my head, split my scalp, bounced off, and landed in the grass. I sat there, my head hanging down and thinking, *ouch*. Then the blood started trickling into my eyes.

American Eagle came over and announced, "You're going to need stitches. Don't wash the blood off. The emergency room serves you faster if you're covered in blood." This was true. As soon as I walked in with my gory mess of a head, they immediately escorted me back to get my stitches. And when they were done they took away my bloody shirt and gave me some scrubs to wear home. When it comes to funny hospital stories, that's all I've got. Hospitals aren't funny. They're designed to fight against death, and that makes them a testimony to the fact that death exists. The most successful operation, the most brilliant doctor, the most miraculous pharmaceutical is nothing but a detour on a one-way street.

"You know what's funny?" I said. "This one time I was helping a wrestler named American Eagle—"

Motorcycle Guy watched me impassively. He put his hands in his pockets and shrugged deeper into his jacket. "Go on."

The icy wind bit like it had the jagged teeth of Mount Hood behind it. The emergency room cast a clinical blue light on the pavement, a small rectangle of artificial light in the too-real night. Beyond the grass was the helicopter pad, a reminder that every minute matters. We waste so many of them without thinking, and at the end an extra twenty seconds can mean the difference between life and death.

I remembered walking through those doors with Krista. The fear, the stress, the unanswered questions of what was happening to her, to us, to our future. I saw Imaginary Jesus walking around the outskirts of the parking lot, his arms folded against his chest as if for warmth, his eyes avoiding mine.

I stopped dead. "I've seen enough of this place."

"You're going to go inside with me," Motorcycle Guy said. "You're going to tell me what happened." He tilted his head toward Imaginary Jesus. "And then we'll talk to *him* about it."

"Okay." I took a deep breath and shuddered as I exhaled. I walked toward the door and it opened with a deep sigh, a sound of profound weariness.

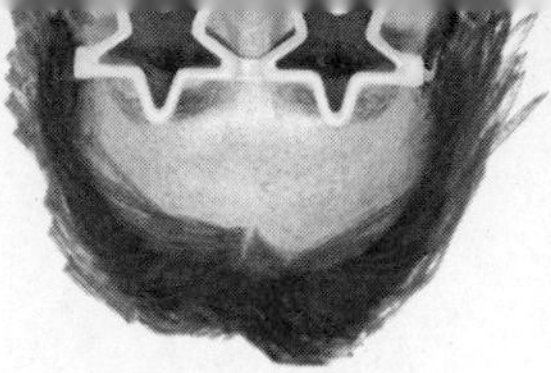

CHAPTER NINETEEN

Death and All His Friends

No one looks up when you walk into a waiting room. No one wants to make eye contact. No one wants to know your story. Our story, like theirs, led us into this room. People were on their cell phones, telling stories to their loved ones. "Of course I'm fine," they said. "No, I haven't seen the doctor yet."

I had been out doing errands with the girls. Krista and I were leaving on a business trip to Thailand the next morning, and Krista, newly pregnant, was tired. I took the kids out more to make an oasis for my wife than to buy anything at the store. As I drove toward home, Krista called my cell phone.

"Hello, beautiful," I said.

"I need to go to the hospital." That was all she said. I dropped the kids off at my parents' house without explanation, and fifteen minutes later we were in the emergency room. It took two hours to get from the front desk to a hospital room.

Krista and I took turns calling our parents. "Mom, sorry I didn't give you much warning before bringing the kids by," I said.

"It's no problem, honey. Is everything okay?"

"We don't know yet. Krista is bleeding. We were going to surprise you in a couple of weeks. She's pregnant." I looked at Krista, whose eyes were already red from weeping. "We think she might be miscarrying, but we're not sure."

Our parents prayed for us. We were glad to know people were praying, because our God is just and loving and powerful. I had been praying since the moment Krista told me she was bleeding, *Dear Jesus, please protect our baby.*

Meanwhile, Krista's cramps got worse.

Finally, the nurse called Krista's name and took blood samples, asked all the questions, gathered the insurance information. We prayed with everything we had. Emotionally exhausted, trying hard to hold on to some shred of hope, we prayed and told Jesus what was happening, because we *knew* he could fix this. The nurse showed us to our hospital room, and Krista started the humiliating process of putting on her flimsy backward shirt. A sitcom played on the television, trying to assure us that life is a comedy, that in half an hour all our problems would be solved.

"I don't want this to be happening," Krista said, lying in the hospital bed.

"Me neither." I held her hand, with nothing more to say.

In a while someone came and took Krista for an ultrasound. I watched that tiny black-and-white screen with desperate hope, searching for the miniscule movements and miniature body parts that mean a baby.

"I'm sorry," the technician said. "I don't see anything."

We already knew, we had known somehow, but we both melted into tears. The doctor came and gave Krista a pill. "For the pain." And she told us that the baby had probably died before tonight, that there was nothing we could have done, that it wasn't our fault.

We stared at the television until the paperwork was done. The baby was gone. Now every place we would go—the hospital, our home, the plane to Thailand the next morning—would be just one more place we didn't have a baby. One more place to fill with tears.

Krista's Vicodin kicked in. "I know our baby just died, but the pills make me feel so . . . *happy*."

I rubbed her arm. "That's why people get addicted to them, I guess."

"I don't like it," she said. "How can I mourn and be happy at the same time?"

Now I turned away from Motorcycle Guy and burst out of the emergency room, running through the parking lot. I could see Jesus on the edge of it, where the last of the streetlamps pooled their meager light. I ran to him and grabbed him by the tunic. I shook him but he wouldn't look at me. "Where were you?" He didn't say anything, and I pounded my fists into his chest. "What happened to 'Ask and you shall receive'? Are you going to say that I didn't have enough faith?" I pushed him down into the grass. "God healed her hands but you couldn't stop *this*?" I could barely speak, the rage was pulsing through my face, hot tears burning my eyes.

Jesus held up his hands to me. "You have such limited understanding, you don't know all that I know."

"I know that she was pregnant. I know that my baby died and that you could have stopped it, that I *asked you to stop it*, and you didn't."

"It's all for the best," he said. "Perhaps the baby had a developmental disorder—"

I kicked him once as hard as I could in the side. "SHUT UP!" I wiped furiously at my face. "I don't care. I would have taken her! I would have loved her." I kicked at the ground. I clawed up some dirt and threw it at him. He covered his face with his hands. "I would have loved her however she had been born."

"Be careful how you speak to me." He stood and pointed at me angrily. "You think you have it worse than other people? You think a miscarriage and a couple of bad breakups make you an example of suffering in this life?"

"Yes," I said. "We suffer and what are you doing about it? I know that other people have it worse than me, how could I not? With all the genocide and war and rape and abuse and children starving, I have it pretty good. But the question remains, *Where were you when my baby was dying*?"

"In this world of sin . . . ," he started, but I furiously waved at him for silence and he, as always, obeyed me.

"The more important question is why I'm even talking to you about this. Because he hasn't answered me, I guess." I pointed at Imaginary Jesus. "Your answers infuriate me. I'm done with you. I want to speak to the true Jesus."

"You're questioning God's power," he said.

"No. I know he has power. If he were helpless, I wouldn't feel betrayed by him."

"You're questioning his goodness."

"I know he's good. I know he loves me. He's proven that often enough. But why didn't he show up on this day? Why did he heal her hands but not our baby?" I leaned against a car, grabbing my chest. I could barely breathe. I heard a screaming child being carried into the ER, and that piercing wail brought tears cascading down my face again. I fell to my knees. "Where is my little girl?"

"She's safe," Jesus said, and he knelt beside me.

I pushed him away. "I don't want your platitudes. I want to talk to the real Jesus, not some fantasy from my own head."

"What would you say to him?" Motorcycle Guy asked.

"I would tell him that if he had been here, my daughter wouldn't have died," I said. "That no one's daughter would ever die. I would ask him how he puts up with Death and all his friends—Pestilence, Disease, Famine. I would ask him, 'How long, O Lord, righteous and true, will you continue to let us suffer?'"

Motorcycle Guy gently put a hand on my shoulder. "You said all those things to him months ago. You said them the day of the miscarriage. You said them on the plane to Thailand. He heard your cry. He heard your questions."

"But he hasn't answered."

"I have one more place to take you," he said.

I grabbed his jacket. "Can you take me to a place where I'll see my lost loved ones? Are you going to show me my grandparents and let me hold my lost child in my arms?"

Motorcycle Guy crouched beside me and said with infinite kindness, "No. Your grandparents are gone. Your little one is gone. They aren't here, just as he—" Motorcycle Guy nodded toward Imaginary Jesus—"isn't here. Anything I showed you would only be a fantasy. They can't come down to you, you must go up to them."

"Just show me their faces," I whispered. But he shook his head and we walked to his bike.

He flipped up his visor and said to Imaginary Jesus, "We're going to Mount Hood."

"I'll meet you there," he said.

"Stay away from me," I pleaded. "Please."

Imaginary Jesus put his hand on my shoulder. "I'm not going to leave you. I'll meet you at Mount Hood."

CHAPTER TWENTY

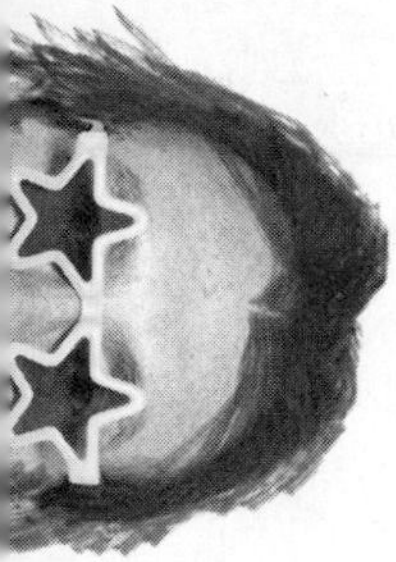

Learning to Listen to Your Inner (Tube) Voice

It's roughly fifty miles down the Columbia River Gorge to Mount Hood. The Columbia moves fast through the Gorge, and the wind howls consistently and hard, making it one of the most popular windsurfing locations in the world. Riding a motorcycle through this area is desperately cold.

I was inordinately pleased when we pulled up the long, winding road to Timberline Lodge just as the sun was rising. It's an upscale, rustic lodge—the type of place you'd see in a 1930s movie, where the beautiful women smoke long cigarettes and wear stylish ski clothes and the men stand around in tuxedos and make snappy comments.

Motorcycle Guy led me past the high-ceilinged lobby, through the wood-paneled hallways, and into an exterior courtyard paved in flagstones with a low stone wall. Beyond the wall were the ski slopes and three thrones made of ice. Imaginary Jesus sat on the center throne, and to his right sat another Jesus who did not smile or acknowledge us, but seemed lost in deep thought. To Imaginary Jesus' left sat a Jesus who seemed more ordinary than my own, and he smiled when he saw us, lifting a hand in greeting. All three wore ski outfits, complete with goggles, scarves, and ski pants.

I grabbed Motorcycle Guy's sleeve. "I don't want to talk to imaginary constructs anymore," I said.

Motorcycle Guy narrowed his eyes and frowned. "Then why do they keep showing up?"

"What do you mean?"

"Whose imagination do they come from?"

I looked at the flagstone at our feet. "Mine, I guess."

"So when you're sitting in a café and Pete walks in and asks some questions and your imaginary Jesus makes a run for it, who made him do that?" I didn't answer. "When he's hiding, who is the one hiding him?" I kept my head down. Motorcycle Guy made a good point. "Haven't you noticed that he shows up whenever you call him? He's not the one on the run. You are." He crossed his arms. "I'll be waiting by my bike."

The center Jesus stood and motioned to me, and I walked over, clenching my jaw.

"Do you have any idea how hard it is to get ski clothes on over robes and sandals?" he asked. When I didn't laugh he said, "Just kidding."

"What's going on here?"

Imaginary Jesus looked at the other Jesuses sheepishly. "I wanted to give you some answers about where God was when your baby died. We're three possible answers. On my right is Meticulous Providence Jesus, I'll be playing the part of Free Will Jesus, and over here on the left is Can't-See-the-Future-Because-It's-Unknowable Jesus."

I sighed. "And we're going to have some sort of debate."

Jesus grinned. "Of course not. We're your imaginary Jesuses

after all. And we know how much you hate debates, so we came up with another solution."

Pete trudged around the corner of the building, a look of utter resignation on his face, crowned with a scowl so deep it was dragging in the snow behind him. Looped around his arms were four inner tubes. "Pete!" I said.

"Kid, I've evicted a lot of imaginary Jesuses, but yours are a special pain in the patookis."

"What's with the inner tubes?" I asked.

Jesus clapped his hands and cheered. "An inner tube race!" he cried. "And the winner will be the answer you adopt about God's providence."

"God's *what*?"

"Providence. How God interacts with people and the world."

Pete lined up the inner tubes at the crest of a small, icy rise. "Let's get this over with," he said. Each Jesus chose a tube and sat on it. Pete motioned for me to get on one, so I did. Pete told me he'd meet me at the bottom, assuming I survived.

He leaned close. "Remember, this isn't some dream. You could really get hurt here. It's not *Calvin and Hobbes*."

"Thanks, Apostle Mom," I said. The great white slope stretched out below us, an impressive expanse of speedy white. I love inner-tubing and was ready to feel the icy wind on my face. "See you in the funny papers."

Pete moved in front of us, slipping on the ice and almost falling before he caught himself. He lifted his hands and said, "Remember, this is a race. The Jesus who reaches the bottom together with Matt is the 'winner' and will get to remain with him. Ready . . . set . . . SLED!"

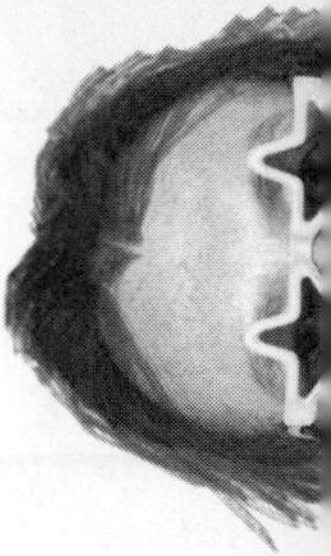

CHAPTER TWENTY-ONE

One Jesus Down . . . Way Down

Our descent started out slowly, and the three Jesuses clumped up near me, each of them hanging on to my inner tube. Someone was dragging his feet, and we weren't picking up much speed. Meticulous Jesus and Free Will Jesus exchanged a glance, and one of them said, "You know, Can't-See-the-Future-Because-It's-Unknowable Jesus isn't even omniscient. We should ditch him now."

Omniscience, of course, meaning that he knows everything. An essential attribute of God, and if what they said was true, then he was definitely not the Jesus for me. I looked over at him just as we hit a small bump in the ice, which accentuated the look of complete horror on his face. "That's not true!" he said. "What an underhanded way to start this. It's just that the future is unknowable because there are free choices to be made that I'm not going to interfere with. I can influence events, and I know what I myself am going to do. I know everything there is to know, anything that can be known."

We were picking up speed now. "Sounds shaky to me," I said.

"Do you see that invisible cat?" he asked. The other two

Jesuses rolled their eyes as if to say, *"The old invisible cat argument."*

I scanned the snow field as we rushed past. "No."

"Because *you can't see an invisible cat.*" Now we were really moving, headed straight for a major bank on the hill. If we didn't figure out a way to turn our motley crew, we were going to go over the embankment, through the trees, and off what appeared to be a sheer cliff. "Look," Can't-See-the-Future-Because-It's-Unknowable Jesus said, "you can choose to turn us so that we stay on the path or drive us through those trees. I'm not going to interfere. I want you to choose. My preference would be to stay on the path. It's the same in life." We were picking up speed. Snow was spraying up from the sides like a puddle being splashed. "I knew your child dying was a possibility. I wasn't certain that was the way it would go. I hoped it would work out differently, but some of the choices in life brought this about. Maybe it was something some company spilled in the drinking water, or maybe your doctor wasn't paying attention, but the thing is, I wanted you to have your choices, and in the end I was saddened by the way it turned out. I didn't want it to go that way, and I am so . . . so . . . sorry."

Can't-See-the-Future-Because-It's-Unknowable Jesus actually had tears in his eyes, and I was touched. He seemed to care, and I knew that it wasn't that he couldn't help me, but that he valued my free will more than my baby's life. Which was pretty lame, come to think of it. And he hadn't known for certain what I would choose before I did? That seemed sketchy.

Meticulous Jesus coughed and said, "Did you see this coming, Can't-See-the-Future-Because-It's-Unknowable Jesus?"

And his leg shot out with a savage kick that sent Can't-See-the-Future-Because-It's-Unknowable Jesus' inner tube careening away from us and into the woods.

As he spun away uncontrollably he shouted, "As a matter of fact, I did, but I hoped you would choose more wisely and—oh no—not the edge, not the . . . AAAAAAAAaaaaaahhhhh!"

Meticulous Jesus and Free Will Jesus both let fly with a hearty laugh, and Meticulous Jesus said, "Ha-ha, that really glorifies me." His savage kick had sent us spinning back on track.

Free Will Jesus laughed, snow caked into his beard. "You sure seem cruel and heartless sometimes, Meticulous Jesus."

"I'm misunderstood!" He frowned at me. "Mikalatos probably doesn't even know what *meticulous* means."

As a matter of fact, I did know what it meant. "It's when you enroll in a school," I shot back.

"That's *matriculate*," Free Will Jesus said. "*Meticulous* means uptight."

"No, it means in control," Meticulous Jesus said. "Nothing surprises me. I cause the sun to rise and the rain to fall on the righteous and the wicked alike. I cause the birds to sing in the trees. I cause the cat to stalk the bird. All these things work together for the good of those who believe in me. All of this works for my greater glory. *Meticulous* means that I'm a God who cares about details."

Just as he finished saying this, we went over a large bump and all flew in the air. When we came down my head hit the ice and Free Will Jesus' hat flew off. "Did you cause that?" I asked.

"Of course," Meticulous Jesus said.

"And what about rape and genocide and babies dying? You cause sin, too?"

"Not exactly." A clod of snow came up and hit me in the face. I brushed it out of my eyes and lost control of my tube for a moment. Meticulous Jesus reached over and steadied me. "Before I made the world I looked at all the possibilities. And I chose to make *this* one, knowing all the terrible things that would happen. Rape, genocide, death, all those things. I don't like them. I knew they would happen. But they are against my will."

"Against your decreed will," Free Will Jesus put in.

"Come again?" I said.

"Against his *public* will . . . you know, don't kill, don't steal, et cetera. But then there's his secret will, where he wants it all to happen so that he gets more glory."

"Your *secret* will?" I asked. "You mean deep down you want all this to happen?"

Meticulous Jesus shrugged. "Of course. This is the best possible world for my end result, which is glorifying myself. People are still responsible for their choices. I merely chose the world where they chose evil. I allow free will, but in a different way than Free Will Jesus."

"The end justifies the means?" I asked. "Is that really what you're saying?" Just then a branch from a tree smacked me in the face. "OW!"

"You had that coming," Meticulous Jesus said. "Since before the foundation of the earth. Show some respect."

Below us the trail split in two, and the Jesuses started jockeying for position. I think each one figured that if he could pull me his way and ditch the other Jesus, that would be the end of the contest. But the trees were coming up fast, and I was headed straight for a big one. "Guys," I said, "you need to let go of my arms." Neither of them budged. They were each yanking and twisting, trying to break me loose from the other. The trees were coming fast. I closed my eyes and prayed, and then realized that my Jesus was right here beside me, just an inner tube away.

"WATCH OUT FOR THAT—!"

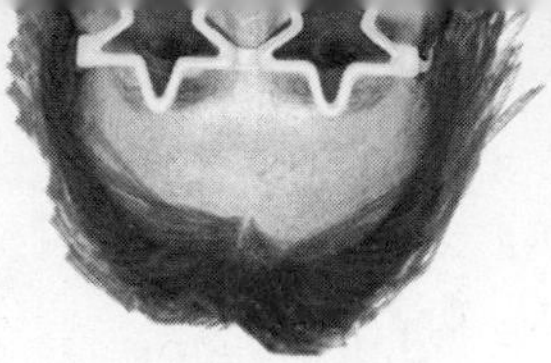

CHAPTER TWENTY-TWO

Oooooooh! TREE!

Both Jesuses looked up and gave simultaneous cries of dismay before letting go of my arms as if in rehearsed tandem. Their release sent me careening straight for the trunk of a monstrous tree ahead of me. "GOOD-BYE, CRUEL WORLD!" I shouted, then curled into the fetal position, determined to leave the world in the same way I came into it.

Luckily (providentially?) a small bump in the ice redirected me and I shot through the trees with unparalleled speed, the snow forming a blind wall of unknowing around me. I could see dim shapes of trees whizzing by on either side and feel the occasional branch smack me in the face or arms. Then I shot up and over the embankment and found myself miraculously and mercifully back on track. The two Jesuses came zipping in from either side of the death forest I had just navigated by sheer plot convenience. They immediately latched on to me again, grinning with those perfect, white, even teeth.

Free Will Jesus smiled gently. "The important point here is that Meticulous Jesus *chose* for your baby to die. He *says* he didn't want it, but he secretly did. This is the best of all possible worlds, he says."

Meticulous Jesus shook his head. "You say it the wrong way. The fact is, when something terrible happens—a cruel, unexpected divorce, for instance—you can say, 'Jesus is in control, he knew this would happen, I can trust him.' If you were the real Jesus," he said, pointing at Free Will Jesus, "they could just say, 'Jesus lets people do evil things to me.' Nice."

Free Will Jesus snorted. "True, I *allowed* your baby to die. Meticulous Jesus *chose* for your baby to die."

"Do you claim responsibility for everything that happens in this world?" I asked Meticulous Jesus.

"Not responsibility. But I did choose this world. In the end I will be maximally glorified by the events of this world, even those things that appear to work against my will."

"My child's death glorifies you," I said levelly.

"Yes. In the end it will."

Suddenly, a giant brown bear came lumbering out of the woods. It scented us, turned, and hustled its ton of fur, fat, and muscle in our direction. "Is that bear chasing us?"

Meticulous Jesus smiled. "Yes. He's starving to death and is looking for something to eat. I arranged for him to scent you to help speed up your choice."

The snow was icy enough that the massive bear could slide toward us, and that's precisely what he was doing, his thick arms spread wide and his lengthy black claws reaching for our tubes. His big black tongue lolled out and a warm cloud of bear exhalation floated over my head.

"Are you insane?" I asked, kicking my feet along the ice in an effort to somehow get more speed so we could put some distance between us and the hungry bear carpet sliding along behind us.

"Which Jesus would you rather have?" Meticulous Jesus yelled. "One that's in control or one that's going to give you a libertarian free choice right now?"

"I DON'T KNOW WHAT THAT MEANS!" I shouted. The bear took a swipe at me again and his paw glanced off my inner tube. Fortunately it was just enough of a shove to send us a few feet out of the bear's reach.

"Libertarian free will," Free Will Jesus said, "means that in any given situation you can choose to do anything you want, and that if you somehow were given that precise same decision again, you could make a different choice."

"On the other hand," Meticulous Jesus continued, "I also believe in free will, but I believe that you choose what you most deeply want to do and that in the same situation you would always make the same choice no matter how many opportunities you are given."

The bear breath was hot on my neck.

"So which way do you want to go?" asked Free Will Jesus. "Who are you going to trust when a voracious bear is trying to eat you?"

The wind whipped through us and the bear growled behind us, scrabbling through the snow and snapping at Jesus' scarf. I didn't know what to do, and the only criterion I could think of was *Which Jesus is least likely to get me eaten?* Free Will Jesus might allow me to make a poor decision that would end with me getting eaten by a bear. On the other hand, Meticulous Jesus might be maximally glorified by a mouthful of steaming Mikalatos entrails hanging from a bear's maw. I reached into my pocket and felt the Frog of Hate and a few coins. I pulled out a coin and held it up for them to see. "Let fate decide." I flipped the coin into the air. "CALL IT!"

"He has freely chosen to flip a coin!" Free Will Jesus shouted.

"He most deeply wanted my meticulous control of all things to decide!" Meticulous Jesus yelled.

The coin described a perfect, shining arc above us, sparkling in the sunlight. I reached up and it descended in slow motion to touch my outstretched fingers, bounce, and fly backward. I leaned for it and my inner tube tilted. The bear's mouth opened wider still and slobber came gushing toward me, the coin, Jesus, and Jesus. As I fell off my tube and slid on my back toward the bear, Meticulous Jesus reached for me and fell off his tube as well. The bear bore down upon us and a mountain of muscle, hair, and teeth overshadowed me. Free Will Jesus snatched me up from the snow and pulled me across his lap. The bear grabbed hold of Meticulous Jesus by the thigh and immediately started to slow himself by digging his thick legs into the snow, which piled up around them.

"METICULOUS JESUS!" I shouted as the bear trotted off into the woods, dragging Meticulous Jesus by the leg.

He raised his chin so we could see his upside-down face. He grinned at us and gave us two thumbs up. "Don't worry. I've got it all under control!" Then they disappeared into the trees.

CHAPTER TWENTY-THREE

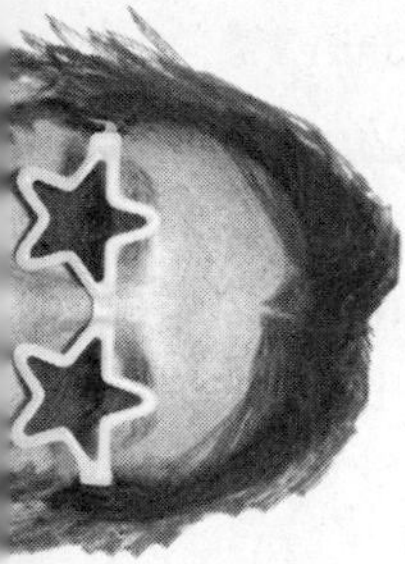

Return of the Frog of Hate

We didn't have time to mourn Meticulous Jesus, because now Free Will Jesus and I were wedged onto one inner tube and our speed had doubled. Tiny figures in the distance rapidly became full-size people stumbling over one another, trying to get out of our way. I grabbed hold of Free Will Jesus' neck and curled myself up tight. A crowd of people gathered at the bottom of the hill, pointing up toward where the bear had been. They had lined themselves up like ninepins.

"Incoming!" I cried. But they didn't move.

"They are choosing to ignore us," Free Will Jesus said. "Isn't libertarian free will beautiful?" At that same moment we plowed through the crowd and they scattered through the air, jackets and hats and scarves and goggles and ski poles flinging up into the sky like a dozen real-life Charlie Browns, and landing in an explosive pattern of discarded clothing and human beings. A nimbus of snowbound bodies encircled us, and another few people piled on top of us.

The inner tube gave the illusion of coming to a stop, but it was still creeping forward. It edged toward another incline, this one leading to the parking lot. I grunted for everyone to get off, but since my lungs were collapsed beneath the mountain of people on top of me, no one gave any indication of having heard me. We were picking up speed. Someone on top of the pile saw our impending doom and leaped to safety. I heard the rumbling of a large truck and tried to lift my head to see better. A snowplow was lumbering directly into our path.

"We're all going to die," I shouted, but it came out as a squeak.

"Insightful and true." As Free Will Jesus said this, we hit the front of the snowplow, scraping all the strangers off my body just as our inner tube finally protested all the violence done to it and popped with a bang and a sigh. We continued our forward motion on Free Will Jesus' rump, but I rolled to the side and slowly came to rest by bumping into a motorcycle at the far end of the parking lot. It was Motorcycle Guy and Pete, both of them leaning against the motorcycle, looking unimpressed.

"So that's your choice," Pete commented. Free Will Jesus lay splayed out in the center of the parking lot, his hair in a haphazard halo around him, snow and mud spattered across his face and chest.

"I guess so. He must be the real Jesus, since he won the contest."

"Nah," Motorcycle Guy said. "You wanted him to win, that's all. I had hoped you might come down the mountain alone."

Free Will Jesus—my Imaginary Jesus—stood up and limped over to us, smiling broadly. "Quite a ride," he said, "but here we are, together again." He helped me to my feet. "You had me worried when that bear came out of the woods." He laughed. "And when Meticulous Providence Jesus kicked Can't-See-the-Future-Because-It's-Unknowable Jesus over the side of the cliff . . . ha-ha . . . Hilarious!"

I raised an eyebrow and considered Free Will/Imaginary Jesus carefully. "You haven't really given a compelling answer about our miscarriage."

"Yes, I have," he said indignantly. "The free actions of moral agents—that's humans—cause bad things to happen. Sometimes I intervene, and sometimes I don't, because if I always intervened, then you wouldn't have free choice."

"So you chose not to intervene, for instance, during the slaughter of the Armenians by the Ottoman Empire, even though many Armenians were Christians? You chose not to interfere when the Nazis killed the Jews?"

"I interfered here and there, but I didn't change the overall shape of things, no."

"You have an enormous capacity for human suffering," I said.

"And you whine a lot about suffering. *Oh, it's so sad. I can't find a parking space. Boo hoo, I wrecked my car, which costs more than most people in the world make in their lifetimes.*"

"So those are my three choices," I said flatly. Up the slope I could see Can't-See-the-Future-Because-It's-Unknowable Jesus being skied away on a stretcher, and it appeared that Meticulous Jesus was being dragged toward us by the bear. I wondered if I would be better off with one of them. I wondered why none of their answers satisfied me.

"Those are the choices *you've* come up with," Pete answered. "Some of them are more theologically solid than others, but the only person who can answer this definitively is God himself. Why are you wasting your time like this? Why don't you ask the real Jesus?"

"I did ask him, Pete, you know that. But he never answered. I guess that's why I invented this guy."

Imaginary Jesus unzipped his snow clothes and stepped out, now in his familiar robe and sandals. He shook his hair out and combed it back with his fingers, then cracked his neck and stretched his arms. "Matt, you designed me to represent Jesus to you. I know now that I'm not real. And even though you're outgrowing me, you made me enough like the real Jesus that I want what's best for you." He dropped his head and rubbed his hands together, his scars white against the snow. "I think it's time for you to let me go."

"What?" I looked to Motorcycle Guy or Pete for help, but they turned their heads away. I stared at Imaginary Jesus, dumbfounded. I had that feeling in the pit of my stomach when you say "I love you" to your girlfriend and she replies, "We need to talk." I wanted to say, "*You're* breaking up with *me*?"

"You say you want to get rid of me, but every time you send me away you call me back. The first problem you face, the first time you pray and don't get an immediate answer, you call me back, your own extrapolated answers to your own questions. You're praying to yourself, Matt. Even an imaginary Jesus doesn't like to see that."

I clenched my teeth and glared at him. I didn't like his implication that *I* was the problem. I had tried to get rid of him, after all. On the other hand, when I couldn't help Pete's sick mother-in-law, the first thing I had done was ask him to come and bring me some medicine.

"I don't know how to stop calling you up," I said. "I don't want to stop calling you."

"The problem is that you honestly like me. You can compare me to the Jesus in the Bible and see that I'm not real. You can compare me to your own experience of the real Jesus and see that I'm a fake. Your own friends point out my inconsistencies. Logic pokes holes in my reality. But time after time, you keep returning to me because deep down *you prefer me to the real thing*."

I nodded. It actually made sense. The real Jesus was frightening sometimes, and he said things I didn't like. He required sacrifice. He scared me by doing things I didn't believe he could. He was a better person than me. I preferred my fake Jesus.

"Remember that time in high school," I said, "when you told me I should start dating Jenny Smith because you said she was hot, and then when she wanted me to sit with her at lunch every day you pointed out that Cheryl Jones was way prettier, so I told Jenny, 'I prayed about it and God doesn't want me to be with you anymore' and then I started going out with Cheryl?"

"Yeah."

"That was fun."

"For you, I guess."

"Remember that time in college when I hadn't studied for biology and you told me it would be okay to cheat because you had created biology and if I ever had questions about it in the future, I could just pray and you would tell me?"

"Yup."

"Do you remember when I saw those homeless people and you told me I could ignore them because they were dirty smelly bums?"

"Sure do."

"We've had some good times," I said, and it was true. I could have listed a hundred other exploits together. He had taught me that I didn't have to tithe when my credit card debt got to be too high and had encouraged me to pick apart my pastor's sermons and criticize my leaders because I was a "good American." He showed me how to find out things that weren't my business by saying, "Is there something I can pray for?" and assured me that I was just like everyone else when I hardly prayed at all. And there were those little unacknowledged moments I could savor when someone I disliked revealed a flaw or inconsistency, and Imaginary Jesus and I could sit back together and talk about how much better I was than them.

"Great times," he said.

"I don't want you to go away."

"I know."

"But at the same time you're not who I really want. I want the real Jesus. I want the startling, bizarre, amazing relationship with the God who created the whole universe, the one who heals my wife's hands in the dark, the one who loves me even though I'm a screwup, the one who sends apostles and talking donkeys and strangers on motorcycles to bring me back to him."

Jesus grabbed my shoulders. "He's not me," he said. "I'm just you. You're a lonely man who talks to himself in the dark."

"How do I get rid of you, then? How do I send you away if deep down I don't want to get rid of you?"

Imaginary Jesus shook me gently. "I think you know the answer to that."

"I have to stop loving you and wait patiently for the real Jesus."

"He's not a lapdog. He doesn't come anytime you whistle. But he never leaves you, either. He's with you right now, Matt."

"I'm afraid," I said. I put my hands in my pockets and felt the Frog of Hate there. I pulled it out. His spots shone in the white sunlight. I knew what I had to do. This symbol of deepest annoyance and pure, undistilled hate was the answer. "Would you like to see this?" I asked.

"What is it?" Imaginary Jesus asked, and he put out his hand. I set the frog in it, and he turned it over, looking at the simple Magic Marker inscription of *HATE*. "Is this . . . the Frog of Hate?"

"That's right," I said.

"I always wanted the best for you," he murmured sadly.

"I hate you," I said, mustering as much conviction as I could. "I never want to see you again." He just stood there and said nothing, the Frog of Hate in his hand. I told Motorcycle Guy to get on the motorcycle and I climbed on behind him. I nodded at Pete as we pulled out of the parking lot, and when I turned to look over my shoulder, I could see Jesus standing there, contemplating the frog. A dark cloud had rolled in, and the first plump snowflakes began to fall. I saw the snow sticking to his hair, his eyelashes, his robe. And he didn't move, didn't raise his hand in farewell. He just gazed at that frog like it was a crystal ball, like it had answers, like it could take him somewhere safe and warm, a place where he wouldn't face the betrayal of his own creator.

I put my face against Motorcycle Guy's back and watched the snow and trees and road and everything I had ever known going past us. A deep pain crawled inside of me, a certainty that the world was broken like so much expensive pottery and that the answers I knew to explain why God could stand there and watch it were neither significant nor sufficient. I asked God why he wasn't answering me, but there was only silence. A melancholy sadness rode alongside us.

By the time we got off the mountain, I was shaking from the cold. Motorcycle Guy shouted back, "We'll stop at Multnomah Falls Lodge and get you something hot to drink." I tried to answer but could only shiver. The world was a cold, dark place. I didn't see any reason why I shouldn't feel cold and dark myself.

CHAPTER TWENTY-FOUR

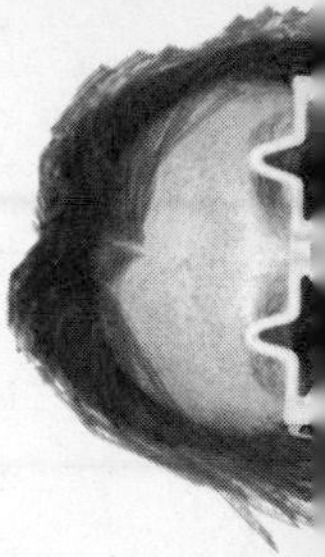

A Burning in the Bosom

Two months passed with no sign of Imaginary Jesus. I hadn't seen Pete since the parking lot on the mountain. I hadn't seen talking animals of any sort, let alone my friend Daisy. I had driven through town once looking for Sandy, but I couldn't remember exactly where she lived, so I settled into life with my wife and daughters again. I waited with skeptical patience for Jesus to show himself. I had begun to doubt that he would. I worked, I read books, I watched television, I hung out with my family, I planned elaborate traps for Houdini Dog

Then the doorbell rang. As always, my girls scampered from their various hidey-holes around the house and looked out the window to shout out what visitor might await us.

"It's two guys!" Zoey called.

"In suits!" Allie added.

I flung the door open to see two young men in black suits. They were, perhaps, twenty years old. They looked like a young Laurel and Hardy. One was skinny and tall, and the other was wide and taller, with dark hair combed forward on his head. "Can I help you?"

"I'm Elder Hardy," the wide one said. "And this is Elder Laurel. We're here in the neighborhood helping people find the real Jesus." *What a coincidence*, I thought. *I'm here in the neighborhood hoping to find him.* "We're from the Church of Jesus Christ of Latter-day Saints." They even had nameplates showing that their names were, indeed, Laurel and Hardy.

"Who are they, Daddy?"

I put my hand on my daughter's head. "I'm not sure. A singing telegram or something."

Elder Hardy scowled. "What makes you say that?"

"Because your names are Laurel and Hardy. That's a joke, right?"

"I don't get it." Elder Laurel scratched the back of his neck. "Why is that funny?"

"Great Caesar's ghost! Could it be that you are so young that you have never heard of Laurel and Hardy?"

The two missionaries put their heads together and talked in hushed tones for a moment. Elder Hardy turned to me and said, "We will ask one of the bishops to explain it to us later."

"We'd like to set up an appointment with you this week," Elder Laurel said.

"We could go for coffee right now." I called to Krista to ask if she minded me stepping out for a bit.

She came around the corner and saw who was at the door and rolled her eyes. "Go ahead. But I don't think they'll want coffee."

I slapped my forehead. "Mormons don't drink coffee, I forgot."

Elder Hardy graced me with a genuine smile. "No problem."

I said good-bye to the girls, and the three of us piled into the cab of my truck. I drove out of the neighborhood and we headed south on Highway 99 toward Muchas Gracias, my favorite Mexican place in town.

Muchas Gracias is open twenty-four hours a day and run by people who have, at one time, lived in Mexico. The Muchas Gracias chain helps establish new immigrants to the States and then teaches them to sponsor more. I am a huge fan of the concept and support the restaurants wholeheartedly with my fast-food budget. The first time I went to Muchas Gracias, the woman taking my order unfailingly referred to me as "ma'am." Now the boys and I quibbled briefly about what to get. Laurel was from Arizona and skeptical of the food. He ordered the carne asada tacos at my recommendation, Hardy went with a chicken chimichanga, and I got a torta.

"Sorry about inviting you to coffee," I said.

"That was funny." Laurel took a bite of his carne asada. His eyes lit up. "Hey, this is great!"

"Best Mexican food in the Northwest. Are you allowed to drink decaf?"

Hardy explained, "It's not the caffeine, it's the tannic acid."

"I didn't know that." I was learning a lot here. Not about Jesus, but about Mormons. "Can you drink soda?"

Elder Hardy placed his arms on the table and leaned forward. "There's a story that someone went fishing with the prophet—the prophet is the head of the church—and asked him if he was allowed to drink a Pepsi, and the prophet said, 'You may drink it, but God prefers that you not.'"

"So it's on your own conscience?"

"Right." Elder Hardy nodded. "But we know that there's something in soda that causes damage to your bones."

I took a big bite of my torta. "So this is all a health thing?"

"That's right," Elder Hardy said. "We're supposed to take care of our bodies and be as healthy as possible."

I paused and considered this. A thought hit me as I watched the boys mop up the food. I said, "Elder Hardy, how's that chimichanga?"

"It's good," he replied, with no apparent awareness of what I was getting at.

"The *fried* burrito you're eating?"

"Yeah, it's good. Real good. I'm full but I'm going to finish it off, I think."

I had tried eating one of those chimichangas once and had spent much of the afternoon trying to counteract the burning in my bosom.

"Anyway," Elder Laurel said, "let's talk about your Jesus and the real Jesus."

"I would like that," I said. "This is going to be fun."

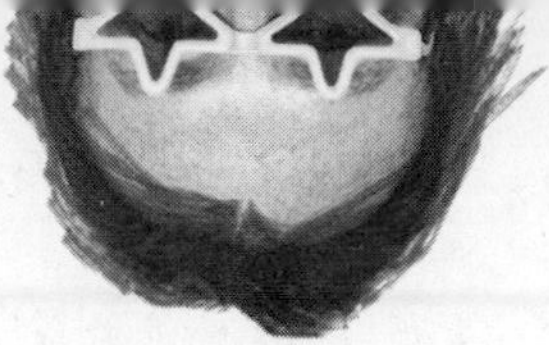

CHAPTER TWENTY-FIVE

Mormon Jesus and My Jesus

Do you know what the best-selling book of all time is? The Bible. The Bible is big business. It sells more than any other book ever, and every year it's the number one book. Bibles are in every hotel room you ever stay in. Many people own multiple copies, and they buy new ones when those wear out. Churches are stacked with them. Bibles are everywhere. No doubt God is extremely pleased that he is a best-selling author and that various new editions and study Bibles are constantly being put out. He did a good job on it took his time and wrote it over several thousand years. It's an impressive book.

The Mormons believe that at a certain point God decided to follow up his enormously successful book with a sequel. Like many sequels, the writing seems sloppier. In fact, large chunks of it seem to have been lifted whole cloth from an English translation of his more successful earlier work. But no one expects the sequel to be as good as the original. I knew that my new elder buddies would ask about it pretty soon.

Elder Hardy started out by saying, "Have you ever read the Book of Mormon?"

"Parts of it," I said. "A long time ago."

"How did you *feel* as you read it?" Elder Hardy asked.

I pushed aside the orange tray with my food on it. "I don't want to offend you."

"Go ahead, be honest."

"I'm a writer," I said. "And most of the time I was reading the Book of Mormon I suspected that someone was trying to copy the style of the King James Bible—"

Elder Laurel eagerly burst in with a comment. "We read the King James Bible, you know."

I thought of King James Jesus' faux pas with the donkey and smiled. "I know. What I'm saying is that I was distracted because it seemed that the style of the Book of Mormon was like someone *trying* to copy King James English but not quite succeeding."

Elder Hardy puffed up his cheeks and blew a half raspberry in annoyance. "You're getting at how there are errors in grammar, things like that. You need to understand that Joseph Smith only had an eighth-grade education at the time he translated the Book of Mormon from the original Egyptian and Hebrew."

"Wow," I said. "I know some Hebrew. That's impressive. How did he translate it exactly?"

"He had two artifacts—," Elder Laurel started.

"The Urim and Thummim," Elder Hardy added. "They're in the Bible, too. Then God supernaturally translated it, and Joseph Smith told people what to write down."

I leaned back in the booth. "So you're saying that God dictated the translation to Joseph Smith."

"That's right," Elder Hardy said.

"So the aforementioned grammar mistakes, those would be *God's* grammar mistakes?"

A long silence followed this question. Elder Hardy furrowed his brow and looked at the cracked surface of the table. I could tell he didn't want to back down from anything he had said. At last he admitted, "That's right."

I couldn't imagine this was correct. Elder Laurel looked uncomfortable. "Elder Laurel," I asked, "is that right?"

"That's a good question," Elder Laurel said.

"Let's move on to another topic." Elder Hardy took another bite of his chimichanga.

"I've got to get home, anyway," I said, so we piled back into the cab of the truck. We were just as tightly wedged in as before, but now a little thicker from our hearty lunch. "So what would be the main difference between what my church says about Jesus and what you say about Jesus?"

"Where do you go to church?"

"It's called Village Baptist. It's in Beaverton." Beaverton, I explained, is just west of Portland. The elders weren't from around here, and although they had biked and walked all over Vancouver, they knew nothing about the Portland area.

"Baptist," one of them repeated noncommittally.

"It's not like you think," I said. "It's a great church. I've had amazing experiences there. The pastoral staff is amazing, and they've created this bizarre community of Koreans, Chinese, East Indians, Hispanics, and Anglos, and they all meet together. The notes are in multiple languages. I've never been anywhere like it."

"The only real difference," Elder Hardy said, "is that your church says that we don't worship Jesus. But we do."

"So you believe all the same things about Jesus as the people in my church do? The Nicene Creed type of thing? Fully God, fully man, virgin birth, lived, died, rose again, rules at God's right hand?"

"Whoa." Elder Hardy held up his left hand. "The Nicene Creed—now, that's different. That was just a bunch of people getting together and voting about what the Bible would say. And we believe in Jesus and Heavenly Father and the Holy Ghost, but not that they are all one."

"You don't believe in the Trinity."

"We believe in the Godhead."

"Wow. I have a lot more questions for you now. True or false: Jesus is God."

"True."

"True or false: There are three gods."

"True."

"What about 'The Lord our God, the Lord is one'—quoted in the Old and New Testaments? It says there's only one God."

"Good question," said Elder Laurel.

I had learned that when Elder Laurel said "Good question," it meant that neither of them had a convincing answer. So I started a new line of questions. "Did Jesus exist eternally, into the past as well as the future?"

"We all existed eternally," Elder Hardy explained. "Matter and energy can't be destroyed. We were all intelligences, and Heavenly Father rearranged things to create us. Jesus is the first being he created."

I stopped the truck. Cars squealed around us. "God *created* Jesus?"

"Yes."

"So the difference between the intelligence that became Jesus and the intelligence that became me is . . . what?"

"He was chosen to die for us, and he became part of the Godhead."

The light turned red. This Jesus who was "just like mine" didn't match a lot of things I understood from the Bible. "So it was like a promotion?" I asked.

Elder Laurel laughed. "You could say that."

"That's pretty different from my beliefs."

"You know, I guess what we teach about Jesus *is* pretty different."

We pulled into my driveway. "Let's get together and talk again," one of the elders said. He handed me the thin blue book that was God's supposed sequel to his international best seller, and they gave me a section to read for our next meeting.

The last thing Elder Laurel said to me was, "It seems to me that you're sitting around waiting for God to show up. There's no reason you can't go looking for him. 'Seek, and ye shall find.'"

I slapped the Book of Mormon against my palm and watched them walk across the street to talk to my neighbor.

Krista came up behind me and put her arms around me. "How was your meeting with the elders?"

"Great," I said. "They're good kids. They have some strange ideas about Jesus, but don't we all? I think that if they would simply open their eyes and try hard to find the real Jesus, they just might see him. I hope they do. They remind me of myself."

And it had been a valuable conversation for me. Elder Laurel had made a good point about waiting around for God instead of going looking for him. I decided that I would do some research and find Jesus here, in the Portland area. He was omnipresent, at least according to my understanding. I wondered if my new Mormon buddies would agree to that. But if he was everywhere, there was no reason that I couldn't find him—the real Jesus—right here in Portland.

CHAPTER TWENTY-SIX

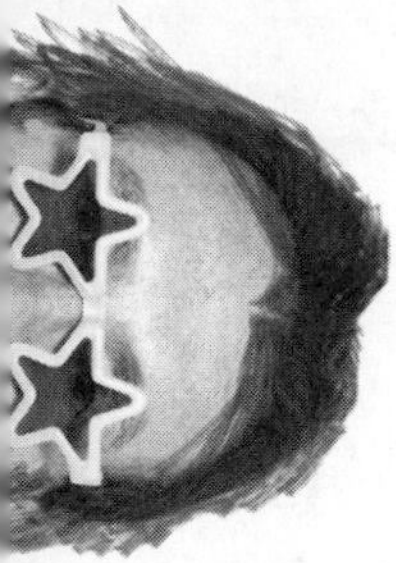

The Atheist Bible Study

One afternoon shortly after my meeting with the elders, our phone rang. Krista answered and talked for a while with the person on the other end. I could hear her laughter filling the house. I went downstairs to see what was so funny, thinking that Krista must be talking to one of her good friends. She handed me the phone and told me that it was "our friend" Sandy. I was pleased to hear her voice.

"Matt," she said, "I've started going to this Bible study I think you would enjoy visiting."

"I'm pretty busy."

"It's an atheist Bible study," she said. "At Portland State University."

I held the phone against my face, trying to process the information she had shared. "I'll be there."

PSU is right in the heart of downtown. City streets cut through campus, and a stranger driving by might not guess it was a campus at all. The atheist club at the school had started a Bible study and invited Sandy to join them so that they could have "the Christian point of view." Sandy had met one of them in a business class she had started taking a few months ago.

The study met in a room on the second floor of one of the buildings on campus. I met a couple of the students beforehand, and they seemed genuinely pleased that another Christian had come to hang out. The atheist students (Mark, James, Nellie, Darren, and Shane) looked like students from any random Bible study on any random campus. There was the kid who looked like an athlete, the big hairy guy who didn't wash enough, the little guy with the glasses, the average-looking guy, and the requisite young lady who was slightly Goth but only slightly.

I was surprised when Shane—the average-looking guy: thin, tall, dirty blond hair—said that he hoped everyone had done their homework. Apparently they hadn't, because they immediately took out their Bibles, cracked them open, and silently read from the book of John. Most Christian students I had been in Bible studies with would completely blow off a question like that with a quick apology. They wouldn't stop talking and actually read their Bibles. Amazing.

I asked Shane why he had started the study. He didn't have to think long before he said, "I believe we should make informed intellectual choices. I realized that I was against Christianity on the basis of what I had heard about it. I was against Christ on the basis of his followers and their idiocies. I wanted to read the Christian Scriptures for myself and truly understand them. In fact, I'm working my way through all four of the Gospels right now."

Today's study was on John 4. We didn't pray before starting, which took me off guard, though it made perfect sense.

We started by reading through the chapter. The unfamiliarity of the story to the people reading it was refreshing. Nellie had never seen the word *sower* and pronounced it like *shower*. Nellie colored slightly and said, "I have no idea what this is saying." The others encouraged her, and someone suggested she try a different translation.

I know you're waiting for an uproarious story of hilarity ensuing at the atheist Bible study, but in fact they showed a real concern for understanding Jesus and a careful patience in studying the context of his words. They had some great insights. Mark pointed out that Jesus' miracles seemed to revolve around health and sustenance and connected that with the continuous metaphors about food and drink.

Darren (small guy with glasses) desperately wanted to make Jesus into a secularist, which is interesting and sad and textually impossible. He spent a long time explaining how the passages about worshiping God in spirit and truth might, in fact, be saying that if people followed reason and treated each other respectfully, a sort of secular utopia could be established.

Shane had little patience for this. "Darren, that's a good thought, but an impossible reading given the context of chapter 3. Remember when he told Nicodemus that he must be born again? He's talking about spiritual truths, not mundane ones. Nicodemus even asked him, 'How can a man get into his mother's womb and be born again?' and Jesus explained that he was talking about the spirit, not physical birth. He's saying the same thing to this Samaritan woman. He's telling her, 'You've looked for satisfaction in physical relationships, but I can give you a spiritually satisfying life.' He says *eternal life*, which can't mean a secular kingdom. He means it literally."

Throughout the evening, Shane offered to let me or Sandy comment on various concepts or passages. We found that we mostly contributed historical background on the story, but Shane was the one who consistently shared spiritual truth by his careful study of what Jesus was saying. He was preaching. I looked around for the strange imaginary Jesuses I had hoped to see in the room, but I didn't see them. Instead, Jesus was merely a dim figure, standing in shadow, a question mark on his face. For Darren, Jesus was a secular philosopher, but even that seemed to be more a projection of his worldview onto the blank slate of his imaginary Jesus. And Shane's Jesus stood at his shoulder, whispering spiritual truths into his ear and then watching them roll about the table. I could see him, transparent as a hologram, flickering, but real.

I realized with a start that Shane's Jesus was not imaginary at all. The real Jesus was in the room in a powerful way. "He's not a Christian," I said to Sandy as we walked away from the study, not sure that was true. The trajectory of his life was shooting inevitably toward Jesus.

"Not yet," she said. "Can you imagine him getting to the end of John without becoming one?"

I thought of Pete, setting out on a path to follow Jesus before he even knew who he was. Shane seemed to have his feet on the same path, carefully studying Jesus and building a knowledge of him that would prove unshakable in the years to come. He was new to the path and I suddenly realized that I envied him. Here I was, with so much more knowledge of Jesus, so many more experiences with him, yet I envied this young man, getting to know him for the first time.

At the end of John 4 we'd read about an official who came to

Jesus and asked him to heal his dying son. Jesus said, "Unless you people see miraculous signs and wonders, you will never believe." Several of my new atheist friends had nodded at that. If they saw miracles, they would believe. But I had seen enough miracles to know that wasn't enough. Sometimes seeing miracles makes the later lack of them that much harder. If he healed the official's son, why did he let others go without healing? "I believe," I said out loud. "But I wish you'd send some more miracles."

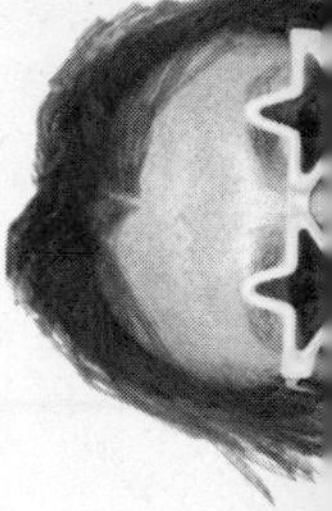

CHAPTER TWENTY-SEVEN

Laurel and Hardy Meet Mohammad

When I pulled into my driveway, Elders Hardy and Laurel were crouched over my sidewalk, white shirts pressed and name-plates on. My dad was working in our front yard. We have a lot of roses, and he's better at caring for them than we are. The elders were hunkered down next to my kids, chalking the sidewalk. Zoey had drawn a reasonable picture of a horse and a shaky representation of her name. Allie had drawn a house with smoke coming out of it and a crooked version of her name. Elder Laurel had drawn a cat and Elder Hardy had drawn an amorphous blob. They, too, had signed their dubious masterpieces: "Elder Hardy" and "Elder Laurel."

Zoey came running to the truck and said to me as I got out, "Dad! See those two guys? They both have the same first name!" I grinned. I liked these guys so much and was glad to spend another afternoon with them.

I sent the kids inside and the three of us decided to walk to Burgerville, just a few blocks away, for fresh strawberry milk shakes. After we got our drinks and sat down, Elder Hardy asked me if I had read the section of the Book of Mormon that they had suggested. I had, in fact, read it. It was a strange passage in which the "lost tribe of Israel" (ancient Jews in Latin America) meets the resurrected Christ. They are pleased to meet him and gather in orderly lines to take turns putting their hands into his side.

"I read it," I said. "And I have a question."

"Go ahead."

"So you have this lost tribe of Israel—Semitic people—and what language was the Book of Mormon translated from again?"

"Hebrew and Egyptian."

"And yet somehow Jesus introduces himself as Jesus *Christ*." They stared at me blankly. I waited for them to put together my question. They just kept staring, so I said, "*Christ* is a Greek word. We would expect that a Hebrew text would say *Messiah*. Maybe it would be translated 'anointed one.' But for a Greek word to show up in the middle of a Hebrew text—that's just weird. And then it talks about baptism, which is another Greek word. Both *baptism* and *Christ* are transliterated from Greek, meaning that they are basically taken over into English without changing them. They're not translated. How do you explain that?"

Elder Laurel said, "That's a good question."

Elder Hardy said, "I don't know the answer to that. But God knows the answer. And if you pray and ask God to show you the truth of the Book of Mormon, I can guarantee he will do that."

I took a sip of my milk shake, giving Elder Hardy a few seconds to collect himself. Then I started again. "The person I'm interested in is Jesus. Who is this Jesus who shows up and talks in Greek to a bunch of Jews stranded in America? He's a god, but he was created by God. He sends a vision of himself to Joseph Smith and then . . ." I paused. Something had just occurred to me, a surprising connection that stopped me in my tracks.

Elder Hardy said, "It requires faith, Matt, we're not denying that. Jesus showed himself to Joseph Smith and gave him the golden tablets to be translated. After that, the golden tablets were taken up into heaven. We have no physical evidence of any of this. You have to trust it's true."

"You know what's weird?" I asked. "Joseph Smith and Mohammad have almost identical stories."

"I'm not really familiar with Islam," Elder Hardy said.

"Allah sent his angel to Mohammad while he was in a cave," I explained.

"Joseph Smith was in a grove of trees," Laurel said.

"Right. And an angel appeared with a vision of a purified religion to both of them. Then Mohammad dictated the scriptures and someone wrote them down." I said, getting excited. "Mohammad was actually illiterate."

Hardy dismissed me with a wave of his hand. "Joseph Smith took the gold tablets and covered his head and read from them as people wrote down what he said."

"He dictated, just like Mohammad."

Hardy pursed his lips and grimaced. "It's not that similar."

"Both the Koran and the Book of Mormon were taken up to heaven," I said. "Both men had multiple wives. There are many similarities. Doesn't that bother you?" I asked. "All the similarities between the origins of Mormonism and Islam?"

He didn't seem concerned. "We would say Mohammad was a prophet too."

My jaw dropped. I had no idea that the Mormons believed this. And maybe that's not official Mormon doctrine—maybe this was a strange heresy of the elder before me and not any reflection on his religion overall. Regardless, I couldn't think of anything to say. I just expressed my wonder by showing my tonsils.

"There's a pattern," Elder Hardy said. "After Christ, about every six hundred years, God sends a prophet. Mohammad was one of those. Joseph Smith also came at the end of one of these six-hundred-year periods."

"Amazing," I said. "What do you mean when you say he was a prophet?"

"That he was a sort of spiritual genius, given insight by the Holy Ghost about spiritual things."

I thought maybe this was the equivalent of Hardy's "God made the grammar mistakes" argument, but when I looked to Elder Laurel, he was nodding.

This stick of dynamite completely derailed my train of thought. "I think this makes God seem schizophrenic," I said at last. "Every six hundred years God gives humanity an entirely different system for interacting with him? The theology of Mormonism and Islam are vastly different. If both Joseph Smith and Mohammad are prophets, then God disagrees with himself pretty often."

Elder Laurel considered me thoughtfully, but Elder Hardy fell back on his Answer to Everything. "You need to pray and ask the Holy Ghost whether the Book of Mormon is true."

"You told me that last time," I reminded him.

"Did you do it?" Hardy asked eagerly.

"No."

He sat back, disappointed. "You really should."

"Have you ever had a moment where Jesus spoke to you so clearly that you could hear the words?" I asked. "Have you ever known he was talking to you like talking to someone on the telephone? And you asked him questions and he talked back to you and told you things you had no way of knowing?"

"No. We're not high enough for God to speak to us that way," Elder Hardy said. "He speaks that way to prophets and spiritual geniuses. Not to ordinary people."

"I disagree. I think he speaks to us every day and we drown out his voice by saying, 'That can't possibly be Jesus' or 'Jesus only speaks to spiritual geniuses' or 'I can't believe that. My parents would be so disappointed if I followed the sound of this voice.' I think we can ask him questions—important questions—and he'll answer us."

"I don't believe that," Elder Hardy said, but Elder Laurel watched me with a curious look in his eyes.

"I believe it," I said. "I believe he's here right now."

Elder Laurel surveyed the room carefully, but Elder Hardy told me that we should meet again in the future. He took out his calendar, and we tried to come up with a time, but I wasn't all that interested anymore. As I walked home I decided to take the next day to walk around Portland and look for Jesus in the midst of the everyday. And it worked.

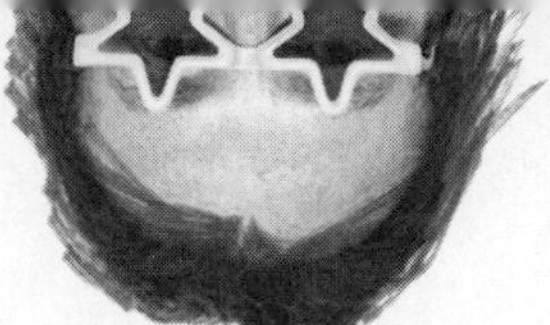

CHAPTER TWENTY-EIGHT

Back in (the Red and) Black

In a mystery novel, detectives are always returning to the scene of the crime. It's the best way to catch a crook. Not to imply that Jesus is a crook or anything, but I thought, hey, I figured out I had an imaginary Jesus at the Red and Black Café, maybe the real Jesus would be waiting for me there. And as I walked down the streets of east Portland, headed for the café, I caught sight of a dusty brown donkey with a white star on her nose. I ran across traffic. The drivers were too used to it to swerve, but they did lazily glare at me. Someone halfheartedly flipped me the bird, but I saw that he had California plates. He hadn't gone completely native yet.

"Daisy!" I said. "Where have you been?"

"I do have other cases I'm working on," she said. "In fact, in a few minutes I need to get over to the convention center." But for now she walked with me toward the Red and Black. When we got there, she trotted up to the window and pointed with her nose at a trim man wearing a checkered shirt, a brown jacket, and a New York Yankees ball cap at a back table, eating what appeared to be a taco salad.

"Is it hard pointing with your nose?" I asked.

She sighed. "You know who I'm pointing at, right?"

"I'm not sure. If you had fingers it would be much easier. Especially this finger," I said. I pointed at it with my right hand. "It's called a pointer finger."

"That's George Barna," she said. "He's probably the most influential living researcher on Christianity and the church."

"Who's the most influential dead researcher? Is it a zombie?"

She didn't laugh. In fact, she ignored me, a good sign that we were becoming close friends. "Some people say he's the most quoted person in the Christian church," she said.

"Huh. Never heard of him."

Daisy shook her mane in frustration. "Just go in there and talk to him."

So I walked in the door and hoped no one recognized me from my earlier altercation with Pete and Imaginary Jesus. Then again, people at the Red and Black were all about revolution, and you can't have sudden, momentous change without breaking a few chairs and knocking some heads into windowpanes. As I got closer to the man with the Yankees cap, I started to wonder if he wasn't imaginary himself. I'd been duped before. And just because a talking donkey tells you something doesn't mean it's true.

So I walked up to him and pinched him in the arm as hard as I could.

"Ow!" Barna dropped his fork and glared at me. His look of annoyance immediately softened into pity. "You must be Matt Mikalatos," he said. "Daisy told me you might do something ridiculous."

"Hey!" I said. "You can see Daisy too?"

"It's pretty hard not to notice a talking donkey." He waved me over to the chair across from him and I took a seat. He took a bite of his taco salad. "This is the best salad I've had in a long time," he said. "The food here is great."

I was shocked. "The chili is awful."

"You didn't do your research," Barna said. "Just over 63 percent of the Red and Black patrons agree that the chili here is mediocre . . . including the cook. But the rest of the food is exceptional."

I didn't have anything to say to that.

"I like it here," he said. "The idea of revolution and revolutionaries is one that's important to me."

I leaned back in my chair. "Daisy seems to think there's some big reason we should meet."

"She said the same thing to me. She tells me that you've been wrestling with an imaginary Jesus."

"It's hard work. And he keeps appearing in other forms. I don't even know if I'll recognize the real Jesus when he shows up. And I feel alone. No one else seems to be dealing with an imaginary Jesus."

He laughed. "Alone? My research shows that 67 percent of adults in the U.S. would say that they have an active relationship with Jesus that influences their life. But only 38 percent would say they're certain that God speaks to them in a personal, relevant way. There's a whole group of people out there who think that God is silent, even though they have relationship with him. What do you think of that?"

I looked down at the table. "He seems silent to me right now. I'm looking for him, trying hard to find him, and there's just this unbearable, empty nothing. Sometimes I wonder if he can even see that I'm hurting, and that I need to hear from him about all this."

George listened to me quietly. I shared a bit more about the miscarriage, and he told me that he had done research into what people thought about God's response to our pain, too. Turns out that most people think God feels our pain with us. But I fell into the category of the 6 percent who just don't know anymore whether he experiences our loss and grief. And I was starting to lean, honestly, toward the 21 percent who say God is aware of our pain but doesn't have any real emotional response to it . . . not really feeling it like I was, like we are.

"Listen," George said. "The core belief of Christianity has to do with this spectacular moment when Jesus overcomes death by the power of his resurrection, and he shows that he is God when he rises from the dead. If God doesn't care about our suffering, why would he be in the process of repairing the world? Jesus said that he came into the world so we could have life, abundant life. He's not a God of the dead, but of the living. You're at a vulnerable place right now, Matt, where you're most susceptible to imaginary Jesuses. You're window-shopping. You need to stop and look at these Jesuses carefully. Test them. Question them. The real Jesus isn't afraid of your questions. The truth is our friend. That's why I do my research, so we can look at what's really happening in the church and society instead of what we wish was happening. Jesus called himself the truth, as I'm sure you know. The way, the truth, and the life."

And somehow I knew that this was what I had come here to hear. Jesus wasn't afraid of my questions, and he's not afraid of the truth. "I think it would be helpful to look at all this research you've done," I said.

"I have a report online," George said. "I'll send you a link."

Daisy was standing at the window, beckoning me with her snout. Boy, hands would sure be useful for her. "Yeah," I said. "Okay, I'll take a look. But I have one more question."

"What is it?"

"Can I try that taco salad?"

And I did. It tasted like heaven would taste if it were in Mexico. And if heaven had somehow run out of meat. I stepped out of my new favorite restaurant and Daisy gave me a long look from her dark eyes. "Let's go," she said. "Pete is meeting me by the convention center to deal with a couple of imaginary Jesuses, and we thought you should tag along."

George stood outside the restaurant and watched us go. "Matt," he called, just as I was barely in earshot. "You'll know him when you meet him. You won't have any question that he's the real Jesus." And he was right. About that and the taco salad.

CHAPTER TWENTY-NINE

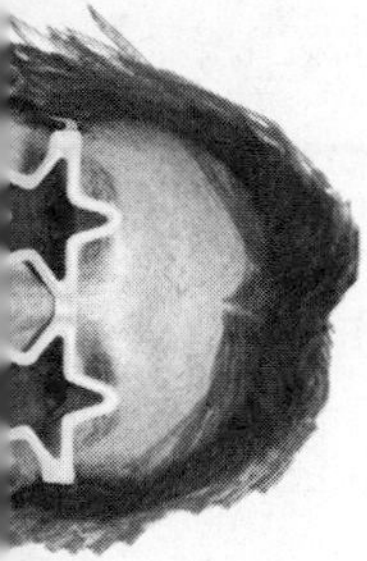

The Parable of Zombie Boy and Werewolf Boy

Daisy and I walked for a long, long time. I had left my car somewhere in east Portland and I knew I'd have to walk back for it, but I didn't want to ditch Daisy now that I had found her again.

"How was your time with George?" she asked. "Was it helpful?"

"Not as helpful as him giving us a ride," I said. "My feet hurt." But we had finally come to MLK Jr. Boulevard and I could see the twin glass towers of the convention center. "So there are some imaginary Jesuses over there?" I asked.

"Yes," she said. "There's a New Age festival in town. There's a huge mess of imaginary Jesuses hanging around across the street there. Pete and I are meeting to try to point out a few of them to the people at the festival." She stopped at the corner and flicked her ears. She tried to hit the crosswalk button with her nose, but it didn't work. "Do you mind?" she asked. I hit the button and we waited for the little white man to tell us we could cross.

"Do you ever wish there was a little white donkey on the crosswalk signs?"

She rolled her eyes. "I don't expect you humans to think about other species."

We walked toward the convention center's entrance. "Speaking of imaginary Jesuses," I said, "you should meet these Mormon guys I've been hanging out with. They have some crazy ideas about who Jesus is."

"Not much different than yours," said a handsome Middle Eastern man on the corner near the MAX stop. He was probably in his midtwenties and he had just handed a sack lunch to a homeless man. He wore tattered jeans and army boots, a collared shirt with a T-shirt over it, and a thick blue jacket on top of that. His hair was black, curly, and chin length, pushed back behind his ears and held in place by a hemp hat. His sideburns threatened to close the shaved space leading to his goatee, but they had been restrained sometime in the last several days. "How is your imaginary Jesus any different than theirs?" he asked.

Despite the fact that I hadn't been talking to him, I said, "Mine was closer to the real thing."

The man laughed. "That's true. Can I tell you a story?"

Daisy didn't say anything, so I answered, "Sure."

He smiled. The homeless man next to him said good-bye and they shook hands warmly. "A man went to buy a new car. The dealer showed him a car made out of stone. It had stone wheels that didn't turn and stone seats that didn't have any give. It had a stone steering wheel. The doors didn't open. The man told him, 'No, I want a *real* car.' So the dealer showed him another car. This one was made out of wood. It was sanded to perfection and painted with metallic paints. The steering wheel turned and the doors opened. Some of the parts under the hood moved. But the engine couldn't start." The man spread his hands wide to me, and then motioned toward the street. I could see the cars whizzing by, headed deeper into Portland. "That wasn't a real car either."

I scratched my head. Daisy had wandered a little ways away and was watching me carefully, her ears flicking. "I don't get it," I said.

"It's a parable."

"I thought parables were supposed to be about stuff that people knew about, like everyday life. And yours was about *cars.* I don't know anything about cars . . . or what that story had to do with anything at all."

"Ha-ha! I can dig that. Here's another story. Are you ready?"

"Yeah."

"Once there were two guys in high school who couldn't get a date to save their lives."

"I understand better already."

"Also, the two boys were a werewolf and a zombie."

"Awesome."

He cleared his throat. "Once there was a werewolf and a zombie in high school who couldn't get a date to save their lives. They were talking in the locker room one day as they cleaned up after PE class. Trying to be helpful, Zombie Boy said, 'If you shaved your arms and back, I think the girls would flock to you.'

"'If *you* wore some cologne, you wouldn't smell like something that just died," Werewolf Boy growled.

"'Maybe if you plucked that eyebrow,' Zombie Boy responded thoughtfully.

"'Maybe if you picked off some of those maggots,' Werewolf Boy suggested helpfully.

"'The problem with you,' Zombie Boy shot back, 'is that you're a monster. Chicks do not dig monsters.'

"'At least I'm only a monster on the full moon!' Werewolf Boy shouted. 'You're a monster every day.' Then they both stormed off. Neither of them could help the other one.

"What do you think?"

I put my hands on my hips and stared at the pavement. "It wasn't really a story," I said. "I mean, no real plot. It was more of a vignette."

"It was a parable," the guy said, sounding slightly miffed.

"Wait a minute," I said. "That sounds a little familiar." I racked my brain, bringing my many years of Christian school training into action. Parables. The net. No. The Prodigal Son. No. Plank-in-the-eye. No. Wait . . . that was it! One of Jesus' sayings to show that you should take care of your own problems before you judge your neighbor. My eyes snapped back up onto the man's face. "Jesus?"

He threw his arms wide, laughing. He gave me a giant hug. "It's about time, Matt!"

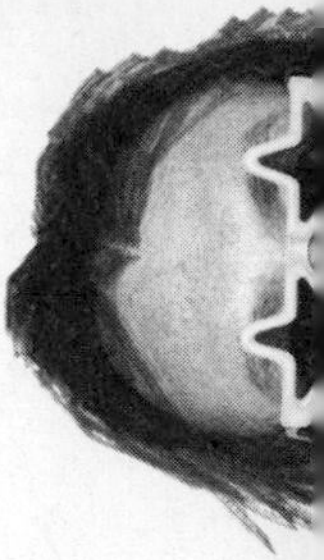

CHAPTER THIRTY

Portland + Jesus = ♡

The next few weeks were glorious. Jesus and I rode our bikes through the forty miles of trails in Forest Park. I pointed out how much I loved the rhododendrons and Jesus laughed and said, "I made the entire Northwest a garden of rhododendrons!" The only things Jesus loves more than rhododendrons in the Northwest are blackberry bushes and moss. He loves moss. He's always draping it on houses, trees, sidewalks, cars, slow-moving animals.

One day, we were eating dessert at the Pix Pâtisserie on Division. Jesus loves that place; he just loves the creative way that the people who work there turn dessert into art. "Edible art," he called it and pointed out the Amélie, which is orange vanilla crème brûlée balanced on a glazed chocolate mousse with caramelized hazelnuts, praline crisp, and Cointreau génoise. It looked like a tiny hat with golden buttons. I had always thought Jesus would be a straight, simple dessert kind of guy, but no. He always pointed out the ones he thought I would like and encouraged me to try them. This Jesus surprised me at last.

"For hundreds of years," he said, "people have had it all

wrong. Thinking I was preoccupied with science. Thinking I was some distant, uncaring, robotic tyrant. Me! Can you believe that?"

"You don't care about science?" I asked.

"I love science. It's ultimately an exploration of my own mind. But not at the expense of art. Look at this place. Look at the yellow walls and those glass cases filled with beauty. And the way the chairs are all clumped together, forcing you to be with other human beings while you eat. I love this place."

"What else have we had wrong?" I asked.

Jesus turned to see the menu on the chalkboard. "Handmade ice cream. You should get some right now. How have you people settled for store-bought ice cream when it's so easy to make your own?"

"That is a great mystery," I agreed. Although I never make my own, I prefer homemade. So I ordered a bowl, and Jesus smiled.

A waitress came over with my ice cream. I took a bite and savored it for a long time.

"Story," Jesus went on. "You've become all about lecture, all about theology. *Boring*. You've vivisected the gospel, and then you wonder where all the life is. The Bible is meant to be interacted with, not cut up on a table."

"I love stories," I said. "I can't always figure out what they mean, but I like them."

"That's another. You think you've got to have all the answers. Why can't there be mysteries once in a while? It's okay not to know the answer." The door opened, letting in a blast of cold Portland air. "There's a friend of yours." Jesus tipped his head toward the entrance.

It was Shane. I would have asked him what he was doing, but it seemed obvious that he had come for the same reason we had—to enjoy the superior dessert. I invited him to sit down, and he pulled up a chair. "Aren't you going to introduce me to your friend?" he asked.

"You can see him," I said. "Very observant! Shane, this is Jesus, Lord of the Universe. Jesus, this is Shane, head of the atheist club at PSU." Jesus shook his hand politely and suggested that he try the Shazam! cake. Shane agreed to give it a whirl. "We're talking about things the Western, modern church has gotten wrong about Jesus."

"Sounds interesting," Shane said. "I have some questions."

"Shoot," Jesus said.

"What is it with Christians and homosexuality? You talk about it more often than anyone I know, even gay people."

The last comment made Jesus laugh so heartily that he knocked my bowl of ice cream off the table. His eyes started watering and he excused himself to get some napkins. When he came back he said, "I agree. There's no reason to talk about that stuff. Someone's feelings get hurt no matter what you say."

"What about abortion?"

"Oh, we've talked about that enough in the last two decades. Give it a rest. Let's talk about something we can all agree on, like eliminating poverty. It's time to show some compassion, not just stand around shouting truth and never showing love."

"That's so cool," I said, beaming.

"The other thing people get all hung up on is that my death on the cross was all about substitutionary atonement. Like the only reason I died was to take away the sins of other people. Does that even make sense? How does my dying make people's sins go away? And what sort of loving father lets his son get killed? I mean, yeah, I had to die, but not because Dad was punishing me for something you did. It's like, 'Dad, Matt stole some cookies,' and Dad comes down with the belt and I say, 'No, no, hit me instead' and God agrees to that? No way."

I nodded, but Shane looked perplexed. "Explain that to me. Because as I was reading the end of John the other night, I saw where you said, 'I, when I am lifted up from the earth, will draw all men to myself.' I started looking at the cross-references and I came to this book in the Jewish Scriptures that said that the Messiah would be pierced for our transgressions and crushed for our iniquities, and by his wounds we are healed. That sounds to me like the very thing you are saying it isn't . . . some sort of substitution in who is being punished."

Jesus tucked his napkin in under his shirt. "Don't get hung up on it, Shane. Let's stop being so judgmental. Let's work on community and learn to love each other. Let's change the way the system works. Let's eliminate homelessness and let's worship with art and music the way we want to do it. Let's allow people to come to church in an authentic way! Wear what you want, have dreadlocks if that's your thing. Let's be who we really are, not try to dress it all up Sunday mornings."

Shane sat back with a skeptical look on his face, a bite of Shazam! halfway to his mouth. I couldn't believe he wasn't buying Jesus' spiel. Shane looked like he was about to talk back to Jesus, and before he could put his foot in his mouth I tried to think of some way to make it clear that Jesus is always right, all the time.

"Let's show Shane what your church is like," I said quickly, before Shane could say anything.

"Okay," Jesus agreed, and we left the restaurant and walked for a while until we got to a residential neighborhood where we found a narrow house with its light on. Jesus knocked on the front door and a kind-looking woman let us in. This was a home group for a new church plant just south of Portland called Corbito Deo, which is Latin for "The Slow-Moving Merchant Ships of God." It appeared that they meant to name the church Coram Deo and got confused. Anyway, inside we were greeted by several young families, some singles, and one old couple. Everyone was sharing food and laughing and talking about life and television and music and art and Jesus. Their kids all had great, creative names, nothing like the kids I had grown up with. The art on the walls had all been done by people from their church, and while it wasn't earth-shatteringly good, it was warm and homey to see something made by hand on the wall. They were doing their best to be "green" and had all arrived in electric cars or on bicycle. They all recycled. They had all voted for change.

We talked about Corbito Deo for a while, too, and the amazing things it was doing in the community—and they truly were amazing. Their tiny group had a great reputation. They had completely painted one of the nearby public schools that had become run-down. They were helping out at the Portland Rescue Mission and a local shelter for runaways. One of the members was starting a new program to help people on meth get clean, sober, and off the streets. We had a great time and had some great conversations, and when we got out on the porch and said our good-byes, Shane seemed to have really enjoyed himself.

"What did you think?" I asked.

"I can see why you're comfortable with this Jesus," he said. I realized this might be *the moment*—the moment when Shane realized that he wasn't an atheist at all, that he believed in God and wanted to follow Jesus. "He's not the one I read about in your Bible, but I can see why you would like him."

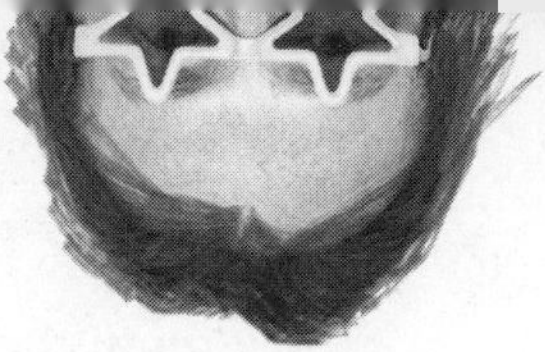

CHAPTER THIRTY-ONE

Stupid Atheists and Their Stupid Insights

Shane's comment hit me like a sack of bricks. "Not the Jesus in the Bible . . . What do you mean?"

He pointed in the window and I looked back at the smiling, wonderful group inside. "How many white people do you see in there?"

I paused. "All of them are white, Shane."

"Well, 10 percent of Portland is Hispanic, 6 percent African-American, 6 percent Asian. Why do you think that group in there is white?"

I thought about it. "It's probably more comfortable for Asian people, for instance, to go to an Asian church."

"Because . . . ?"

"Because . . . I don't know. Jesus, you want to help me out here?"

Jesus was standing on the sidewalk, watching us and smiling. "Oh, the Asian church is all about authority and our church is all about independence in community."

Shane shook his head. "So the Asians go to an Asian church. And the African-Americans—"

"You know, there *is* an African-American guy at this church."

"How many people in the church?"

"The home churches tend to be twenty or less, but they have a larger sort of association that's about three thousand."

"How many black people?"

"One."

"And where are the rest of the black people?'

"At the black church, I guess."

"And where are the Hispanic people?"

"The Hispanic church."

"And Corbito Deo is the—?"

I dropped my head. "The white church."

"That's right. And why are the people there so fun to be with?"

"They're like me," I said. "They like cool music. They care about social justice and the environment. They're young."

"The culture of this church is not mainstream," said Shane. "But it's mainstream Portland."

"Are you saying that this church is just a cultural modification of Christianity?"

"I'm saying your parents and grandparents were modernists and so they wore suits to church. They sang hymns in the fifties and praise songs in the seventies and now they are stuck in the eighties or maybe the mid nineties. And this church—" he jerked his thumb toward the house—"that you think is some new thing that's going to change everything is really just you counterbalancing toward what you like and care about and believe. Some of it balances out the excesses of your parents' and grandparents' generations, and some of it is new errors that your kids are going to balance out. Your daughters are going to want to get dressed up for church when they grow up, I bet. They're not going to want to sing the songs you love from the early twenty-first century."

"But all the service projects and community outreach . . ."

"That's today's American culture. Movie stars flock to Africa. It's hip to adopt. It's cool to care about the environment. This church is more culturally flexible. You're adapting to the needs of today, and that's great. Our atheist club has some similar programs."

"So you're saying that this isn't the real Jesus, either."

"Wouldn't he care a little more about people of other ethnicities and making them feel comfortable in church? You don't have any. You don't even have much age differential in the church. So much for diversity. And you do all this outreach in your neighborhoods, which is great, but as I understand Jesus' instructions, he wanted people to go to other countries, reach other ethnicities, to get out there to people who are different than you. This Jesus doesn't seem to care."

"You have to admit the story part is good, though," I said. "Wouldn't it be great if someone wrote a sort of semiautobiographical novel comedy thing instead of a Sunday school lesson for once? Wouldn't that be cool?"

"Of course," Shane said. "Stories are great. Jesus told a lot of them. But he did lecture, too. You might have heard of the Sermon on the Mount. It wasn't a story. And a lot of the times after a story, Jesus took the disciples somewhere private and gave them a didactic explanation. Jesus liked story, but he also taught in lecture. A good teacher doesn't box himself into one mode of transmission. Deal with it."

"I can't believe I am getting schooled about Jesus by an atheist." I turned and looked at Jesus, standing there under the yellow streetlight, a misty rain falling on his hemp hat and curly black hair. "As for you, I thought I told you to stay away from me. I don't want any more imaginary Jesuses in my life."

I stepped down toward him, and he had a mischievous look of pleasure in his eyes. "But you keep calling me back," he said.

"Not anymore." I took another step toward him. But before I could grab him, he bolted and sped down the road. I raced after him, and Shane ran alongside me. Jesus turned a corner into a dark alley and we darted after him.

Ten minutes later, panting and out of breath, I told Shane I couldn't run anymore. We walked back to where I had parked my car near Division. "My . . . new . . . imaginary . . . Jesus," I panted, "wears . . . Converse. Can't . . . catch . . . him. Need . . . Jesus . . . with . . . sandals . . . next . . . time."

Just then a white Honda Fit turned in front of us. Jesus was driving. "Hey!" Shane shouted. "Jesus hot-wired my car!"

"Into . . . the . . . truck!"

We leaped into traffic and followed Jesus. Jesus, always conscientious about traffic rules, politely turned on his turn signal, so he was easy to follow. He drove slowly toward downtown. He took a strange, meandering route, and we found ourselves right at the entrance to Chinatown. Then, unexpectedly, he turned left and headed west on Burnside.

"He's headed for the highway!"

"He already passed a highway entrance," Shane said.

As Jesus pulled up to the corner of Burnside and Tenth Avenue, he held his head out the window, as if carefully studying the giant kinetic tripod sculpture to our left. He almost threw us off, but not quite, because his blinker was still on and he turned right in front of Powell's Books. Powell's is the largest privately owned new and used bookstore in the world, taking up an entire city block, four levels and nine giant rooms. They've painted the walls of each room a different color and named the room after the paint job. It's the coolest bookstore in the world.

We followed Jesus down Tenth, but he abandoned Shane's car at the corner of Tenth and Couch. (In honor of Portland's slogan "Keep Portland Weird," we pronounce this word "cooch" as in "coochie coochie coo.") Jesus was on foot, running west on Couch. I put the truck in park in the middle of the street and ran after him.

"What am I supposed to do about your truck?" Shane yelled.

I ignored him and ran after Jesus. Jesus slowed for a minute when he saw the homeless man at the entrance to Powell's, selling the *Real Change* newspaper. He pulled out a dollar and gave it to the man before ducking into the bookstore. I skidded up to the doors and flung them open, but Jesus had already disappeared up the stairs, and I followed him into the stacks of the Pearl Room. Powell's is called the City of Books and it's an apt description. Jesus had found a good hiding place.

I walked into the room and started up and down the aisles between stacks. Nothing. Art, music, drama, film. A few Jesuses loitered around in there. Dali's distant and noncorporeal Jesus. Various Easter-movie Jesuses. I walked down the stairs to the Red Room and was immediately surrounded by a throng of clamoring imaginary Jesuses. I thought I saw mine slipping toward the health books. I ran down the aisle after him.

CHAPTER THIRTY-TWO

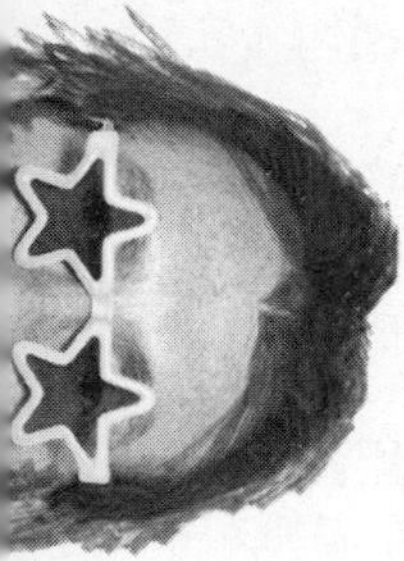

Oh Yes, Jefe, You Have a Plethora

New Age Jesus came flying up alongside me and tackled me. "You left both my chapters on the cutting room floor," he snarled, his purple haze burning my eyes with the scent of too much incense.

I pushed him hard and he rolled to the side. I jumped to my feet and assumed a defensive stance. "You're nothing like the real Jesus. The whole New Age movement would be better off saying they don't believe in Jesus at all. Just ignore him if you can't explain him away. I had to cut your chapters because you were such an easy target you made me look like a jerk for attacking you."

A swarm of denominational Jesuses trampled New Age Jesus in their hurry to get to me. Catholic Jesus and Protestant Jesus argued the whole time. Baptist Jesus was dragging an enormous bathtub full of water behind him. The various Orthodox Jesuses were carrying tasty treats from Russia, Greece, Romania, and all over the world. Stern Jesuses, laughing Jesuses, Emergent Jesus and Emerging Jesus (like good and evil twins, I guess . . . but I can never remember which is which), a few Jesuses who barely fit the description like Universalist Jesus (dressed like Buddha, six arms like Shiva) and the six-inch-tall Bahai Jesus, and all of them wanted a piece of me. Health Nut Jesus came running out of the health section wearing tennis shorts and a headband.

I pulled away from them all and raced into the Purple Room, the mob of Jesuses on my heels. A few more Jesuses from the archaeology section joined us. One from the 1800s was strenuously disagreeing with another from the 1970s about whether the Hittites existed. A Jungian Jesus came barreling up from the philosophy section, Political Jesus and all his friends came from the politics section, and then the Military Jesus crowd joined in, loudly declaring their passionate approval of whoever was victorious in war. Gay and Lesbian Jesus came along too, assuring us that he didn't care about sexual orientation and that he would gladly talk about it to the exclusion of any other topic.

There must have been fifty of them now, babbling, yelling, pushing, shoving. I ran down the stairs to the Rose Room, where the scientific Jesuses marched behind us, doing their best to prove their own existence. "Scientific evidence proves that Jesus exists and is God!" they shouted. Perpetually Angry Jesus shouted them back down. In the back of the crowd someone had found Feminist Jesus, and she was biting Patriarchal Jesus in the shoulder. He yowled in pain but wouldn't hit a woman in public.

All of the children's book Jesuses swarmed around us, their strange, incomplete stories and simplified theology shining through their white, simple faces. Their scars were hard to see, but they loved children and had a consistent message.

"Obey your parents!" one of them screamed, while Liberation Theology Jesus screamed in frustration, "Parents should not create a lesser, unempowered class out of the children!" We burst through the automotive section and, like water spewing through a pipe, shot into the Orange Room.

CEO Jesus came running toward us, saying I wasn't organized enough with my time and didn't I want Jesus to bless my business. Feng Shui Jesus offered to rearrange my house so that the spirits would be pleased, and Cooking Jesus grabbed me by the arm and said, "If you follow my first-century dietary tips, you can live a long and happy life!" I shook him frantically and shouted, "You only lived to be thirty-three years old!"

We crashed like a tidal wave into the Gold Room. Some of the superhero Jesuses popped out of the graphic novel section in the Coffee Room: Super Jesus and Godman. "We're strange visitors from another planet," they cried. "Let us use our superior powers to help, you poor, backward earthling. Your primitive emotions and tiny problems baffle us, but we'll help get the cats out of your trees."

I tried to run through the Gold Room, but that's where the mysteries, erotica, science fiction, and fantasy are kept. Aslan the Jesus Lion roared when he saw me. Alien Jesuses who want us to worship them waved their tentacles. Da Vinci Code Jesus pushed others aside, his convenient inability to see objective reality causing him to foam at the mouth and scream obscenities at Catholic Jesus. They were on all sides of me now, all clamoring for my attention, all angrily demanding that I respond to their questions, their needs, their desires. I was getting Jesus claustrophobia.

Footprints Jesus came up alongside me in the Blue Room

and offered to carry me because he could see I was having a rough time. We wedged ourselves into the Green Room, and there on my left, past the Jesus Action Figures and the New Arrivals, where new Jesuses are manufactured every day, was the Northwest section. And there was Portland Jesus waiting for me, looking through a book of pictures of the Pacific Northwest. He looked up when he saw me. Another Jesus stood beside him, partly in shadows.

I was completely hemmed in by Jesuses. I tried to turn around but I couldn't. A sense of dread fell on me as the Jesuses fell silent. I could see the exit onto Burnside and Tenth. It was across the room, but it might as well have been on the moon. I tried to move for it, but the Jesuses purposely blocked the way.

A figure stepped out of shadows, a diabolical smile on his face. It was Imaginary Jesus. "Now we have you where we want you."

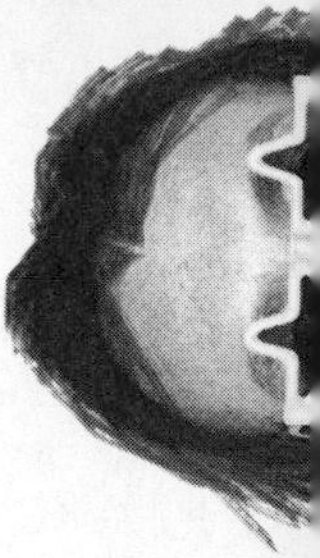

CHAPTER THIRTY-THREE

It Takes a Village

"You," I said.

"*Us.*" He pointed at Portland Jesus. "He and I, we're the same, just in different outfits." When I stared at him dumbfounded, he said, "Like a Barbie doll."

As if to prove the point, Portland Jesus stuck his hand into his pocket and pulled out the Frog of Hate. I looked at it and then up into his face. "How could you do this to me? I wanted to bike on Sauvie Island. I wanted to go to the Humble Administrator's Garden. I wanted to go to the Portland Zoo and ride the train and laugh at the polar bears together. You betrayed me."

"You betrayed us," he shouted. "You give us your friendship, you create us, sometimes you act like we're God." His face twisted into a sneer. "Then you start some ridiculous quest to find the real Jesus. He doesn't exist. He was a man who lived and died and stayed dead, and now all that's left is you playing shadow puppets."

"That's not true!"

"Join us, Matt, and we can rule all of Portland together."

"No! I'll never join you!" I tried to make a run for it, but they stopped me easily, seven or eight Jesuses pinning my arms to my side.

"I guess our only solution is to destroy you," Imaginary Jesus said, but before he could explain the strange ontology of imaginary beings killing real creatures and the likely ramifications, the sound of an enormous bar fight broke out near the door. Suspecting angry businessmen just come from the cash-only Red and Black Café, I didn't turn at first. Then the sound reached drunken punk band levels and I turned just as it escalated to polar-bears-being-chased-by-jet-planes decibels.

Pete stood near the entrance, straddling a large pile of defeated Jesuses. He had another by the robe in his left fist, and his right fist was destroying the milky white teeth of a Model Jesus. His left foot lashed out like justice, and then he flipped into the crowd, walking across their shoulders, heads, whatever got in his way before he descended into their midst, jabbing, biting, and kicking. He grabbed two of them by the beards and knocked their heads together. "Come on, kid!" he shouted. "This is fun, but I'm not doing it all day!"

Imaginary Jesus lunged for me, but I slipped away and ducked past Football Jesus. Then I saw Testosterone Jesus, who was watching the whole thing with a bemused expression on his face. "DOGPILE!" I yelled, and Testosterone Jesus' face lit up. He started stacking Jesuses like cordwood. I jumped into the gap he had created and passed Pete, who ordered me to get out the door. As I skidded onto the pavement I saw my truck. Shane must have driven it partway around the block and left it here on the street. A police officer was writing a ticket for it.

"Not again!" I ran and jumped in. Daisy came flying up

like brown lightning and leaped into the bed of the truck. The officer handed me a ticket and told me I had come just in time, that he had been about to call for a tow truck, and that my friend Shane had jumped into his own car and left this one idling in the middle of the street. I thanked him just as Pete ran out, threw himself across the hood, and jumped into the passenger seat. I hit the gas as the Jesus mob burst out of Powell's. Farmer Jesus had handed them all pitchforks, and Caveman Jesus had discovered some torches.

I cranked the wheel hard and got us going west on Burnside again, and before long we were on the highway, the angry sound of imaginary Jesuses fading into the distance. Pete directed me toward Highway 26 and I shot toward the tunnel that led into Beaverton. "I think we lost them," I said, but then I looked into my rearview mirror and saw something skimming above the pavement, gaining on us like a missile.

It pulled alongside us, a Jesus in dark robes riding on a broomstick, a lightning scar on his forehead. I pushed the truck harder and Daisy stumbled in the bed, braying for me to watch out. Broomstick Jesus bashed into the side of the truck and we scraped up against the wall of the tunnel. "I'll get you, my pretty!" Jesus cackled. "And your little donkey, too!" I hit the brakes hard and he flew past us, but as he did, the sparks from his broom landed on the hood of my truck. Without warning, flames began to shoot up.

"Look out!" Pete yelled.

"Fire!" Daisy brayed.

"AAAAAAAAAH!" I lost control of the truck as we exited the tunnel and careened off the canyon wall. The truck burst into flaming protest, and Pete and I jumped out the driver's side. We helped Daisy get down from the bed, and then we ran a little farther up the highway.

Daisy shook herself, dust and ash flying off her coat. "Get on," she said. "We can't walk the next few miles." Pete got on first, and I got on behind him. Daisy began to run, the sound of her little hooves on the pavement ringing out across traffic. I looked behind us and could see an army of Jesuses coming through the tunnel, driving cars, flying, running, walking on water. A wind started, powerful and impossibly strong. The hood of my sweatshirt tried to strangle me, and I tucked it underneath my jacket.

"Some sort of weather Jesus," Pete yelled back to me. Ahead of us, an SUV lifted from the road and crashed onto its side. "Hang on tight. Daisy's going to run us through it!" Daisy reared up and pushed headfirst into the storm—in one rain-soaked, wind-whipped minute, we had crossed it. I could see the Murray exit ahead, the exit that led to my church. Daisy ran up the off-ramp and turned left. It looked like we were in the clear.

But as we crossed the overpass, an enormous Jesus lifted himself up beside us, his monstrous hand large enough to crush us. He bashed the overpass with a single blow and the ground shook, cracks forming on the pavement. "Ignore him," Pete said, and Daisy leaped over a crack as the ground shook again. We weren't far from my church. I could see the sign from the exit: Village Baptist Church. As we rushed into the foyer, Pete pulled the glass doors shut behind us. "They're coming fast."

A sign over the entrance to the auditorium said Prayer Labyrinth. Our worship pastor, Dean, had announced that Village was hosting a prayer labyrinth this week. I wasn't sure what it was, but they had cleared out all the pews in the main sanctuary to make room for it. I hadn't been planning to go into the labyrinth. Daisy nudged the door open with her nose and slipped into the darkness beyond.

"I don't like labyrinths," I said to Pete. "It's like a maze . . . of prayer. It sounds simultaneously terrifying and boring."

"What's to be afraid of?" Pete asked.

"Well, this one time I went in a maze for Halloween and it was supposed to be scary but it wasn't, and the walls were made out of black garbage bags, and we came around this one corner and there was a vampire with his cape made out of black garbage bags with his back to us so I didn't see him until he turned around and said, 'I vant to suck your bloooooooood!'"

"There are no vampires in a prayer labyrinth," Pete said.

"Okay, well, I also saw this move, *Labyrinth*, in which there was a bad guy who was the Goblin King and he was played by David Bowie. Creepy."

"David Bowie is not in the labyrinth."

"His hair was so white and . . . blow-dried. And he had on this weird purple outfit." I shuddered. "And he walked on the walls."

"Empty your pockets," Pete said.

"Why?"

A shuddering blow came against the glass door and I could see the Jesuses pressed up against the glass, straining to get in like bargain shoppers on the day after Thanksgiving. I quickly emptied my pockets and handed the contents to Pete. I grabbed for the door handle and Pete hissed, "Take off your shoes!"

I kicked them off and slipped into darkness. I felt a jostling behind me, as if others had pushed their way in with me, but as the door shut the last glimmer of light went with it, and I couldn't see anything. I waited a moment as my eyes adjusted to a darkness so deep it glowed a warm, purplish red. A diffused aura of light came from the entrance to the maze, and an arrow in masking tape pointed the way. I walked toward it and plunged into the narrow passageway, my fingers trailing along the walls. "Hello?" I said. "Daisy? Scary vampires? Jesus?" But there was no answer, just the sound of strangers moving nearby in the dark.

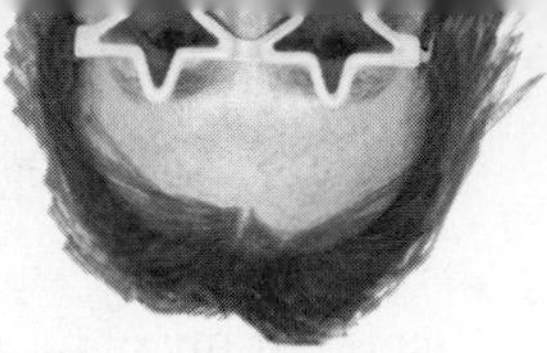

CHAPTER THIRTY-FOUR

In the Labyrinth

Despite Pete's assurances, I suspected foul play in the labyrinth. It was dark, and experience told me that vampires attacked people when they were alone in the dark. Well, not experience exactly, but my friend Television had told me about it often enough. Luckily I had read quite a few fables in my time and I knew what to do.

"Vampires," I said quietly, "I know you are lurking there in the dark, waiting to pop my jugular." I listened quietly for a response, my left hand covering my neck. "But I have something to tell you. There are some other people behind me in the maze, and they have way better blood than mine. If you attack me, they'll hear and run away, because I will scream like a little girl." I paused again and listened. Silence. "I eat a lot of garlic," I told the darkness. "My wife roasts whole heads of garlic and I eat them like candy."

A light flickered ahead of me. A familiar, bluish light. A television. I hurried down the hallway and entered a small chamber, about ten feet in diameter. A television set was propped up on the ground, playing only static. I knelt down and put my hand on the side of the television. "Poor TV," I said. "Are you only able to pick up analog signals?"

"That's you," a voice said from the darkness, and I jumped up into what I hoped was a terrifying kung fu stance. "Why are you standing like that?" the voice asked. She stepped out into the light. It was Daisy. "You still looking for the bathroom?"

I collapsed in relief. It was only a talking donkey. I lovingly caressed the television. "What do you mean when you say that this noble device is just like me?"

"I mean that your head is full of static. Stuffed full of television and radio and comic books and noise. You say you can't hear Jesus, but it's because you have earbuds in all the time. You're afraid of silence. You're afraid to let even a strong signal through."

I frowned. "I'm not afraid. I get bored."

"Tell me about your workout routine," Daisy said.

"It's not really a routine as such. It's more of a workout exception."

"Nevertheless, what do you do when you go to the gym?"

"First I ride the stationary bike."

"Why the bike?"

"So I can read at the same time. Of course, four televisions are on, and I can plug into the sound, so I keep my headphones handy. And the gym always plays oldies for some reason, maybe because Krista and I got a discount to join the senior citizen gym. So sometimes I listen to my own music."

"So for that half an hour you read, watch four televisions, and listen to music."

"I would surf the net if I could figure out how."

"No one is that bored," Daisy said. "You get in the car and

turn on the radio. You take a book with you to the bathroom. You listen to your iPod while you do yard work. You watch television and write on your blog at the same time. When exactly is Jesus supposed to have a conversation with you?"

"If he talked, I would listen."

Daisy shook her head. "No, Matt. He is talking. You're not listening. You're trying to avoid him by filling up your every moment. You need to clear some of the static."

As she spoke, about ten people crowded into the room. I looked around. They were my Jesuses, the ones I listened to or spent time with most consistently. Portland Jesus was there and Legalist Jesus from way back when and Freedom Jesus who doesn't care if you sin because he's so forgiving (I met him when I ditched Legalist Jesus) and Judge Jesus and Foxhole Jesus and Binary Jesus and several others.

"These came from different places. Lies you've believed." Daisy pointed her snout at Unforgiving Jesus. "Lies that someone told you or you told yourself. Some of them are diabolical, and some are self-inflicted. A few are even well-intentioned. They're constructs that tell you what Jesus will say or do, how he feels, what he thinks, without ever having to get to know him."

I looked at them carefully. I had been working so hard to be rid of them, but here in the dark they brought a sense of security. I could turn back now and emerge into the light and never worry about all this again. If God wanted to break through with a message, he could do that. He had done it before.

"What happens if I go deeper into the labyrinth?" I asked her, straining to see through the darkness beyond the television set.

"He's in there," she said. "He's waiting at the center of the maze to talk to you."

I thought about this for a minute, my fear battling it out with my desire to see the real Jesus and get some answers. I knew that if I walked away now, I'd be back in a few months, trying to work up my courage again. I couldn't run from the real Jesus forever. "Then I'm going to go deeper."

"First you should sit here quietly," she said, "and try to hear the signal through the noise."

I sat down with my back to the television, facing the dark. I closed my eyes and listened. A million thoughts rushed into my head and I tried to set them aside as I struggled to listen. "God," I whispered, "cancel all this static. I want to hear you."

I could hear the high whine of the television set beneath the sound of the static. I reached over and clicked it off. I could hear Daisy breathing beside me and the restless shifting of the imaginary Jesuses, who didn't need to breathe at all. And somewhere beyond that, I could hear a distant voice, an echoing whisper from within the labyrinth. It said, "Come."

My eyes snapped open and I looked around me. Only three of the Jesuses were still standing there. Portland Jesus, his hands in his pockets. Legalist Jesus, the oldest of them, with his rules and regulations. And my own personal Jesus, my old friend. A Jesus of comfort and religion. Traditional but funny. Challenging enough to give the impression of being real, but accommodating enough not to demand actual change in my life.

Daisy smiled at me. "You're down to three, Matt. All those hundreds at Powell's, all children of your brain. And now you're down to these three."

I grabbed her head and scratched behind her ears. "Thank you."

Without a word, she trotted off into the dark, back the way I had come. I stood at the edge of the dark hallway. The terminating line between the chamber and the darkness seemed like a precipice. Without a backward glance, I stepped in.

CHAPTER THIRTY-FIVE

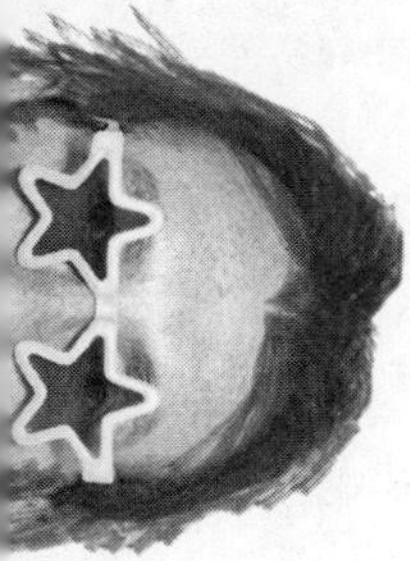

Holy Mother of God

A woman sat at a small wooden table, her gray-streaked hair pulled back in a knot. She wore jeans, a plain blouse, and a cross around her neck. A simple meal lay on the table in front of her: meat, bread, and wine. Pete sat to her left, his legs folded under the table. He looked tired, but he smiled when I walked in. Jesus and Jesus and Jesus trailed behind me, silent.

I sat at the table. Pete took a sip of his wine. There was no plate and no cup in front of me. "I wanted to introduce you to someone," he said to me. "She and I are having Communion. The Lord's Supper. The Table. The Passover meal."

"I'll take it with you."

"No," he said. "For you, Communion is tiny, tasteless wafers and a little plastic cup full of grape juice. Someone reads a few verses, you swallow the bread, you throw down the juice, and you think to yourself, *Jesus, thank you for dying for my sins.* You put the cup in the pew holder, and you're done. Later someone comes by and cleans up the leftovers."

I thought to protest, but I honestly didn't see anything wrong with the way he described it. He clearly disapproved, but that was basically what Communion meant to me. Jesus had said, *"Do this in remembrance of me,"* which meant aren't we lucky to be saved, and we spend a minute making sure we're not sinning, because that would be insulting after he died for us and all, and then we drink our sip of juice, eat our nibble of bread, and we're done.

"What do you think 'Communion' was like at first, Matt?"

I shrugged. "I've never thought about it, I guess."

"That first year after he died, do you think we threw back our cups, took five minutes to say thanks, and then moved on?"

He made a good point. I could spend more time than that reminiscing about a good meal. "Probably not."

"We knew him, Matt. He changed our lives. Our thankfulness wasn't some theological construct. It was deep and true and unstoppable." He paused and put his thick hands on the table in front of him. "This is my dear friend Mary. She would like to show you what it means to do this in remembrance of Christ."

Mary smiled at me, the lines around her eyes crinkling up. "I could tell you so many stories," she said. "I wish you could have seen him when I first held him. Do you have children?"

I nodded. "Two," I said, but tears came to my eyes when I said it. I blinked them back. *Two living.*

"Then you know that when you hold your first little baby, the whole world changes. His fingers were so small, and he cried when he felt the cold air of the stable—it was the purest sound in the whole world. When we took him to the Temple for his dedication, an old man named Simeon came to us and started praying and praising God. He took hold of Y'shua and told us, 'This child is destined to cause the falling and rising of many in Israel, and to be a sign that will be spoken against, so that the thoughts of many hearts will be revealed.' Then, as if in an afterthought, he said, 'And a sword will pierce your own soul too.'

"Of course we had no idea what that meant, even though the prophetess gave similar testimony that same day. But we had seen the angels. Have you seen angels?"

"I don't think so," I said.

"'Don't be afraid,' he commanded me, but I was terrified! And we had seen the shepherds crowding in around the manger, all wanting to touch him, and I didn't want them to hold him. He seemed so tiny and vulnerable, and they were rough and filthy and they stank. But Joseph said, 'He isn't ours alone, Mary. He'll never be ours alone.'" She stopped and took a small drink of wine. Pete put his hand on her shoulder and gently encouraged her to go on.

"One day when he was twelve, we thought maybe he was with his friends. We were all traveling in a caravan, and at the end of the first day's journey we went to look for Y'shua, but he was gone. We raced back to Jerusalem and spent *three days* searching for him. All of the worst possible thoughts tormented me in those three days. Finally, Joseph found him in the Temple teaching the teachers. Those old, learned whitebeards, bowed in careful thought as our son explained the holy words to them. I was so afraid when we couldn't find him—my heart like a frantic bird in a cage—and I kept pushing my breastbone, as if to keep it in with my hands. When we found him, I was amazed, and proud, and so *angry* that he would do that to us. I thought, *This is what the old man meant when he said a sword would pierce my soul.* But I was wrong."

"I can't imagine that," I said. "I guess it would be like some twelve-year-old kid going to a pastors' conference, and all the pastors gathered around him in the hallway to hear his insights."

"He was a boy. They had high hopes for him, of course. He could be a great teacher, they said. They wanted him to move there, to live in Jerusalem. But Joseph said, 'He's of the house of Judah, and firstborn. He's to be a carpenter, not a priest.' But the way the men deferred to him, the way they leaned forward to hear his high voice read the scrolls, it reminded me of when the kings came to us, when Y'shua was a boy." She smiled, and her eyes focused on the middle distance. Pete leaned toward her and again touched her lightly on the shoulder. "'A great king,' they said. The words the magi spoke about him encouraged us deeply. Everyone always had something to say about him.

"It embarrassed me sometimes. What people said." Her chin set forward, her jaw clenched down. I suddenly remembered that he had been born before she and Joseph married, and that the names he might have been called by others were not polite ones. "Sometimes when he was speaking, and all the people were talking about him, people would say, 'Mary, control your son.' And I tried. But do you know the moment that broke my heart?"

I shook my head.

"When they had him on that cross. It was my baby boy, and I couldn't recognize him. Y'shua's friend, John, had to tell me which cross was his. His face was battered and swollen, and blood was caked all over his sides, his arms, his feet. And when he pulled himself up to breathe, it made the most horrible noise . . . like he was drowning." She stopped and wiped at the tears pouring down her cheeks with the palms of her hands.

"I'm sorry," I said.

She didn't seem to hear me. She just talked on. "I was standing below the cross in that horrible crowd. People jeering. Throwing stones, throwing insults. John was standing beside me, holding my arm. Y'shua's good eye moved back and forth over the crowd, and I thought he saw me. His eyes were so swollen, I couldn't tell for sure. But he said, 'Dear woman,' and I looked up at him. He smiled, and his mouth was bloody and horrible. 'Here is your son.' John looked up to him, what was left of him, and he spoke to John. 'Here is your mother.' And John took care of me after that." She wiped at her face. "One of the last things he said, broken and dying. *'Take care of my mother.'* In the midst of his pain, in the center of his suffering, he stopped to take care of me." She fidgeted with her hands and whispered, "A sword that pierced my soul." Her fingers came upon the cross around her neck and she jerked back, as if startled. She held it up for me to see, and it caught the dim light and flicked sparks into the dark. "Do you understand how painful it is for me to wear this?"

Pete broke the bread and handed it to her. "This is the body of Christ," he said, "broken for you."

She wiped the tears from her eyes and smiled at Pete. "Thank you, Simon." I looked at the three Jesuses, and they flickered like the flames of candles. "And the cup," she said, taking a sip, then placing it in Pete's hands.

He took the cup and walked off into the darkness without a word. I stood to follow, and Mary reached out and touched my hand, her skin wrinkled and warm. I looked into her eyes and she smiled at me. "God be with you."

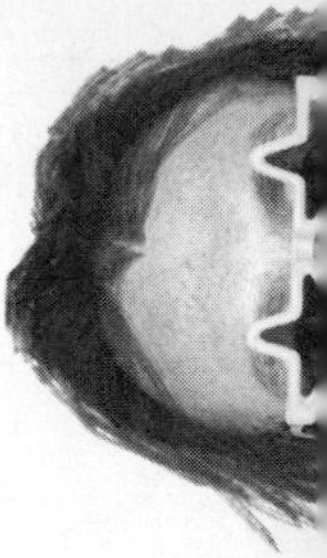

CHAPTER THIRTY-SIX

Dinner with the President

I was walking down a dark corridor with Pete and Legalist Jesus. I didn't see the others. Legalist Jesus said, "I don't know why you expect God to show up. You haven't been good enough for that."

"On the night when we betrayed him," Pete said, "Y'shua met with us to eat together. We called it Passover then, of course. The room had been prepared by the man who owned the house. But there were no servants there to wash our feet." Pete asked Legalist Jesus, "What would you have done in that situation?"

He shrugged. "Ordered one of the disciples to do it."

"Jesus took off his clothes and washed our feet. My friend John says that this was the moment when Jesus showed us the full extent of his love. Not by coming to Earth as a baby. Not by dying. But rather that moment in the upper room, washing our feet. He says that Jesus did it because he knew he had come from heaven, that he had all authority in heaven and on earth, and that he was returning to heaven."

Legalist Jesus scoffed. "He knew he was all-powerful, so he washed your feet? I don't think so."

Pete turned toward me. "Do you understand this?"

"I . . . I'm not sure."

"Look," Pete said, and he pulled open a door on the wall and stepped through. I followed him and found myself in my own kitchen.

Krista looked at me, and she was clearly unhappy. "I told you this would happen one day."

Just then three men in black suits with a giant dog walked through, the dog carefully sniffing at every surface in the house. They moved down the hallway and into the front room.

"What's going on?" I asked.

"The president of the United States is coming to dinner," she said incredulously. "Because *you* invited him. What is wrong with you?"

"Oh no."

"Oh yes," she said in her best I-told-you-so voice.

I had been inviting the president to various family events for as long as I could remember. I had invited President Clinton to our wedding. I had sent President Bush birth announcements for our daughters. I liked to keep the executive branch updated on our family. Krista always said, "What are you going to do if the president shows up for something one of these days?" And I would assure her that this would never, ever happen.

But it had.

Krista gave me a lengthy list of chores to get our house ready. I needed to lecture the kids on correct manners when conversing with the president and his family. I needed to get the neighbors to move all their cars to make room for the presidential caravan and news vans. I needed to clean the bathrooms and mop the floors.

I dove into the work because we didn't have much time: the president was coming to dinner at seven. I mopped the floor, I got the neighbors to move their cars, and I offered drinks to the Secret Service, which they politely refused.

I grilled some steaks on the barbecue on the back porch. At one point, Krista called me into the house, wondering if we shouldn't have salmon instead. We talked about that for a minute, and then I looked out the window and saw that the hood of the barbecue was standing open. I was sure I had closed it. I ran out and the steaks were gone. I could see slight claw marks in the muddy grass, as if some animal had sped away from the scene with terrible speed. I went to the fence and could see one set of marks there, as if claws had touched wood for the briefest moment. "Houdini Dog," I said. He must be a magnificent animal. I had turned my back on the grill for only a few moments and he had come over the fence, lifted the barbecue hood, snatched six steaks, and gone over the fence again. I shook my head in wonder. "Salmon," I told Krista. "Let's have salmon."

Then came the knock on the door. The kids crowded by the window. "DAD!" Zoey yelled. "IT'S THE PRESIDENT OF THE UNITED STATES!"

"SHOULD WE OPEN THE DOOR?" Allie yelled.

Krista had made a feast. Salmon and butternut squash risotto, homemade bread and green beans from our garden. She looked gorgeous in a red dress, her hair up. The president complimented her and our home, and he apologized that his wife and children hadn't come on this particular trip.

We sat down to eat, and the meal went great. The president loved the food, and he made conversation easy and enjoyable. I was in the midst of convincing him which rock bands would be best to have at the White House for his daughter's birthday party (either The Autumn Film or Switchfoot, of course), when a creeping sensation started up the nape of my neck. I had forgotten something important. Something that would make my wife furious if she realized that I had missed it. I started to look around the house nervously.

"May I use your restroom?" the president asked.

Horror bled into my heart. I had forgotten to clean the bathroom, and Krista had specifically told me to make it a priority because the kids had tracked mud and grass into the guest bathroom earlier in the day. What could I say? *We don't have a restroom? It's broken?* I wondered how long I could buy myself by giving directions to the hall closet instead of the bathroom.

"I forgot to clean it," I blurted out, figuring that Krista couldn't kill me with so many Secret Service agents in the room.

An agent stood between the president and the bathroom. "I wouldn't go in there if I were you, sir."

"Why didn't you clean it?" the president asked the agent.

The agent cocked his head sideways and stared at the president through his dark glasses. "It's not my job, sir."

The president smiled. "You know," he said, "I have all the power of the executive branch of the most powerful nation in the world. And I came from my seat of power in Washington, D.C., and I know that in a little bit I'm going to board *Air Force One* and return there. And because of all those things, I'm going to clean your bathroom for you." We sat in stunned silence. He stood up and started loosening his tie.

"Mr. President," I said, "there's really no need for that."

He loosened his tie. He unbuttoned his shirt and pulled it off, then his undershirt.

"Sir, I would rather you didn't," I said.

But he was down to his boxers now. He handed his expensive suit to the Secret Service agents, and before we knew it he was down on his knees scrubbing our toilet.

My wife looked at me with weary eyes that said, *How is it possible that I have married a male version of Lucy Ricardo?* I laughed nervously. Sorry, my love.

The scene faded with the sound of a door shutting. Pete and I stood in the dark hall again. "Washing feet was servants' work. And yet there he was, wearing only a towel, wiping the grime and the dirt from our feet." He leaned against the wall. "What bothered me later was that he knew we would betray him. When I told him, 'I'll never leave you, Y'shua, even if they come with swords, even if we all end up on crosses outside the city,' he simply said, 'Peter, before the rooster crows you'll deny three times that you even know me.' As he poured the water over my feet, he knew that in a few hours I would call down curses on myself and swear that he was a stranger."

I thought about that for a long time. "It wasn't about things you had done, or good behavior. It was just—"

"Just that he loves us," Pete said. "He didn't wash our feet and then follow up with a list of rules. He said to us, 'Now that I, your Lord and Teacher, have washed your feet, you should also wash one another's feet.' Every time I refuse to serve and love those around me, I am saying that I am better than Christ, better than God."

Legalist Jesus stood nearby, nervous. I asked him what he had to say to all this, and he shook his head. "God doesn't love us when we disobey him."

Pete grinned. "You know who was in that upper room with

us, getting his feet washed? Judas. The traitor. Jesus showed him love too. Not because of anything Judas had done, or would do, but despite those things."

And in that moment, Legalist Jesus flickered again, guttered, and finally went out completely, like a flame snuffed in darkness. He was gone. Pete took my arm gently. "He won't be back," he said. "If you focus on this story of Christ and remember what he has done for you, the temptations to bring Legalist Jesus back into your life can be overcome."

A voice came to me again out of the darkness—that strange, whispered, echoing voice, calling me deeper into the labyrinth. One simple word: "Come." I walked deeper without stopping to see if Pete would follow.

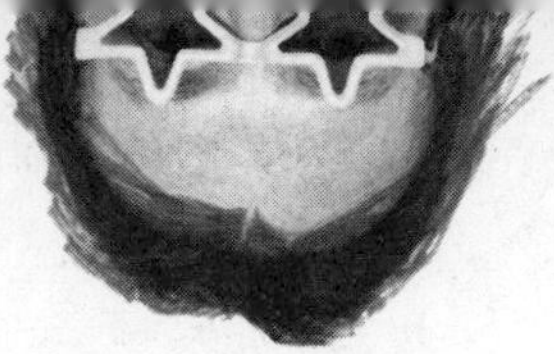

CHAPTER THIRTY-SEVEN

The Center

My two remaining Jesuses stood on either side of me, their arms linked through mine. "You don't have to go in there," Imaginary Jesus said. "We can still go back the way we came."

I pulled my hood up over my face. The whispering voice ahead beckoned me, calm and clear. The passageway narrowed, and as I pushed myself through, I felt Imaginary Jesus' grip on my arm loosen. I turned sideways to try to fit through the crack. I could see a room beyond, brilliantly lit with candles, but I couldn't quite fit through. I exhaled all my air and wedged deeper in. Portland Jesus lost his grip. I could feel him grabbing at my sleeve. I was wedged in and not sure I could move forward. I forcibly exhaled all the air in my lungs and for one terrifying moment I thought I still wouldn't make it, but with one last push I fell into the room. Imaginary Jesus and Portland Jesus stood on the other side, dimly lit and motioning for me to come back. I couldn't hear their voices. It was deathly silent.

This chamber, the largest by far, had a dais in the center with various levels built onto it, each laden with piles of bread and goblets of wine and grape juice. I knelt in front of it and silently considered what sat before me. Jesus said the juice was his blood and the bread his body and that he wanted us to eat and drink it in remembrance of him. I usually did this with other people. I had never been in a place like this and taken it alone.

I took a piece of the bread in my hand. "In remembrance," I said. And I remembered many things he had done for me. My family came to mind. My parents have been good parents, and they would be quick to say that this is because of their friendship with Jesus. My parents-in-law would say the same thing, and I had to admit the blessing that had come with having parents and in-laws who get along so well. That must come from Jesus too, I knew. The way Krista and I had met was obviously more than coincidence. I remembered so clearly the moment when I knew I was falling in love with her. I had tricked her into a date, and as we drove the streets of San Francisco she bit a grape in half, put the halves on her eyes, and grabbed my arm so I would look. Then she shouted, "My eyes! The acid is burning my eyes!" I thought, *I could love a woman like this.* She was beautiful, and not just her eyes, or the curl in her hair, or the way she walked, or the million other pieces of beauty that added up in her every motion and curve. She was beautiful inside, too, in a way that I had seen in few people. I don't think she has ever told a lie. She gets nauseous just hearing them. She's the kind of person who speaks only the clearest, most certain truths, and she's unswervingly faithful in relationships. And she would lay that virtue at the feet of Jesus, because he said, "I am the Truth." The fact that this exceptional woman—beautiful, funny, intelligent, moral, and deeply spiritual—would meet some guy working at a comic book store and even consider him as a possibility was nothing short of miraculous.

I could walk through my many friends, of course, and my sisters and brother. I could mention my daughters, like some mirror image of our child lost to miscarriage. Zoey had been breech, the umbilical cord wrapped around her neck. The doctors tried everything they could to get her turned around, but nothing worked. In the end they performed a C-section and she came to us healthy and well. She has grown into a young lady of surpassing brilliance and charm. She thinks she's a horse, she reads books without ceasing, she writes stories, she teaches me new things about life. It could have so easily gone another way.

When Krista was in labor with Allie, our second daughter, the doctor noticed that Allie's heartbeat became erratic with each contraction, so another C-section was necessary. The hole in Allie's heart was big enough and noisy enough that the medical interns crowded into our room to listen to it. A heart specialist took a look after she was born and told us to wait, so we did. The hole closed up by itself without surgery, without incident. Allie is a ball of giggling energy, a ballerina, a singer, a comedian, a cuddler, an irreplaceable part of our family.

An unending stream of blessings attributable to Jesus came to mind. Our house, the people at our church, the way he had walked me through changes in my own life and taught me to be a better man, the power he had given me to overcome evil around me and in my own heart. All of this without taking into account the stars, the intricate veins on a leaf, the complicated biology of a single cell. All these things were from him too, all these things were worthy of remembrance, of thankfulness, of praise.

And then, of course, there was this bread. His body. I took the bread and dipped it in the cup. His blood. I put it in my mouth, chewing carefully. Here was a reminder that when I least deserved it, when I was his enemy, he died so that I could live. He died so that the entire world order could be restructured, so the dead could live, so that the universe could be restored. He died so that I could live a victorious life, so that I could become like him and no longer be held captive to my own nature and desires but could instead break out of those for my deeper desires, those amazing, wonderful, transcendent actions that I so badly wanted to do but couldn't without his help. He died so that I could live his life.

As I finished the bread, I saw a thousand ghostly images of others around the table, taking the bread and the wine, praying, eating. All of us—fishermen, comic book retailers, construction workers, emperors, prostitutes, Turks, Greeks, rock stars, garbage collectors, people of every possible race, people from remote tribes and monstrous cities, elderly and youthful, the exceedingly rich and the inconceivably poor, all of us following this one man. Not because of who he was once upon a time, but because of who he is today, and because of who he promises we can become. Because he has promised us life overflowing and an end to pain. Because he has the words of life that lead us to God, that lead us to himself.

Moved by this procession of the ages, I took another piece of bread, a larger one this time, and I ate and drank together with my brothers and sisters from across time and space. As they slowly faded, I felt someone behind me place strong hands on my head. I didn't move. I still had my hood on, so I could only see directly in front of me, but I knew whose hands they were. Fear and awe welled up from within me, and a strange sensation of privilege that he would choose to show himself to me in this way. His hands—although I couldn't see them—felt real. Not imagined. Not hallucinated. They were his real hands.

"Don't be afraid," he said. And he prayed for me. He prayed a blessing over me, a prayer for strength and protection, a prayer that I would do the things that he had set out for me, a prayer for courage and hope and deeper relationship. "You have a question for me."

The question seemed different now. It had been about justice. It had been about being wronged, and about where God had been while I was hurt. But in the light of all I had just seen and remembered, the question seemed almost . . . petty. I felt his encouragement, though. I knew that he stood ready to answer.

"If you had been here," I said, "my baby would still be alive." I couldn't bring myself to say it as a question. *Where were you? If you love us so much, how could you let this happen?*

Jesus was silent for a long time, his hands still on my head. I felt him lean down near my ear, and then he spoke quietly. "I am the resurrection and the life. Belief in me brings life, even if you die. And for those who live and believe in me, they will never die." He paused. Then he asked me, "Do you believe this?"

Did I believe? If I didn't believe that he had power over life and death, why would I be angry? There would be no point in being angry at a powerless God, because it wouldn't be his fault that he couldn't intervene. My anger and pain, then, were actually evidences of a deep certainty that Jesus has power over life and death. I believed with all my heart that he could bring life into any circumstance. I simply didn't understand why he had chosen not to do so with my child. The *otherness* of someone who has power over death suddenly hit me. Here was Jesus, God in the flesh, who had come to earth not to condemn the world but to save it. To save us, his creation, the world and people he had brought into existence merely by desiring it. And here I was, a few decades old, thinking I could tell him how to save us. Who was I to say such things to him? I couldn't even help an old woman overcome a fever.

Back in the synagogue he had said that he had come to bring healing to the brokenhearted and freedom for the captives. And we had been told from our earliest ancestors that he would come and do away with sickness and death and pain and take us to live with God. A sudden certainty washed over me that my child had entered into his presence in a more profound way than even this moment when he stood here physically beside me, his hands on my head. She was safely home in a way that I was not. And now he stood near me asking if I believed that he was the resurrection—the ultimate defeat of death. Did I believe that he was the answer to every pain-filled question I had?

"Yes, Lord," I said, "I believe that you are the Christ, the Son of God, who was to come into the world." Then my story spilled out of my mouth as I breathlessly shared it all with him—the bleeding, the hospital, the ultrasound, and the deep loss echoing in the empty places of my heart. When I had spoken it all, when it had poured out until I had nothing left to say, I felt his hands tremble. I heard a sound, as if he had been about to speak. A catch in his breath or a broken word. I paused to hear what he would say. But he didn't speak. Instead he began to weep.

Jesus' tears fell with mine. This wasn't some distant power.

He was hurting with me. He mourned our loss. Whatever his control in the situation, however he had chosen to act or not act, I knew he hadn't made that decision lightly. I felt a fundamental shift inside of me, like tectonic plates grinding back into place. The sorrow hadn't left, but the anger drained away.

We talked for a long time in that small chamber, the candlelight flickering over the bread and wine. I remembered my imaginary Jesuses and I looked through the narrow crack in the wall, but they were gone, done at last. I hadn't said good-bye to them and I was glad, because they were less than a shadow of the real Christ. They were a ghastly insult to the true Jesus. I took another piece of bread and dipped it in the wine and ate it slowly. I could see that another dark corridor led from this room, presumably back to where I started.

"I don't want to leave."

"You can't live the rest of your life here," Jesus said, and his voice sounded kind and amused. "An ambassador never remains in his home country for long." He removed his hands from my head. "My followers must live in the world. My message is for the world, after all."

I pulled my hood back and tried to catch a glimpse of him with the corner of my eyes. I was worried what I might see. If I saw nothing, what would that mean? And if I saw him, would I be able to handle that? I turned, slowly, but I didn't see him. I could feel him near me still, like when someone walks up behind you and you haven't turned to see their face, but you sense them. A certainty of his presence—a stir of air, maybe, or the lingering memory of his hands on my head. "Do you have something more to say to me?" I asked him.

"It always has to be something new with you, doesn't it?" he asked, and I realized how true this was. I wasn't satisfied with the insights he gave me through the Scriptures, the Holy Spirit, and my prayer times. It wasn't enough to hear from his messengers in church or to see him revealed in nature. I wanted more moments like this one—these rare, inexplicable visions. But even as I thought this I realized it was a difference in kind, not in quality. I've had mystical experiences many times in prayer, when his quiet voice has shaken me with his truth. The Bible, prayer, church—these were places where he met with me often and spoke clearly.

I could see it was time to leave. A sense that time had stopped receded from me, a feeling that the world was rushing back into this room, that life—or what passed for it—was starting up again. I could sense him moving away down corridors I could not see. At the last moment I remembered one more question I had for him and I yelled, "Jesus! Did you write the Book of Mormon?"

I could hear his laughter as if from another room. Deep, unfettered, joyous laughter that clearly said, *After all this time, don't you know me better than that?*

I shrugged. "I didn't think so," I called. "But I did promise Elder Hardy I would ask." I stood up and looked around the chamber one last time. I wished I could stay but knew that even in that act of devotion and desire I would be moving away from Christ, not toward him. So I stepped out of the chamber and followed it back, out from the center, out toward the world.

CHAPTER THIRTY-EIGHT

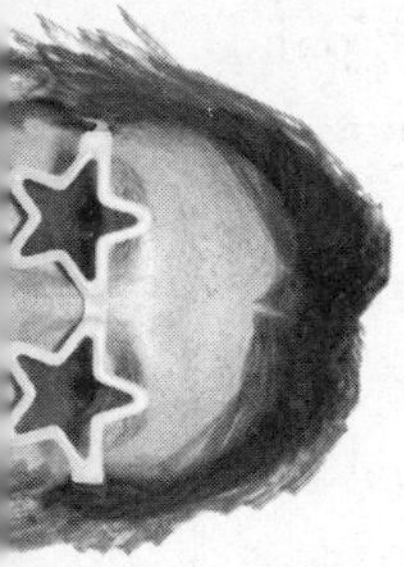

Craft Time with the Apostle John

A feeling of increased reality overcame me as I followed the path. Or rather, increased normalcy, because the encounter in the labyrinth's center had seemed more real than anything I had experienced in a long time. I came around a corner to one last station. An old man, maybe the oldest I had ever seen, sat behind a table. He looked like one of the Muppets, those old men who sit in the balcony and make fun of the show the whole time.

"You've come through the labyrinth."

"Yes. I'm Matt." We shook hands. His felt cool and papery, and when I looked closely, I could see the faded evidence of tattoos across his skin, what appeared to be a densely written script.

"I am John." He held his palm out to the table and I could see a bowl of water, a set of paints, some modeling clay, and some paper. "Sometimes I've found that after being with him these things can be helpful. It's hard to describe your experience to the people out there." His hand waved vaguely toward the exit.

I sat across from him and picked up some of the modeling clay. It bent easily in my fingers and rapidly took shape. If the clay had been responding to my natural ability as a sculptor, I would have rolled out a long, skinny snake, but the clay seemed to respond instead to the complex emotions of my experience in the center of the labyrinth. Within a few moments the clay had formed into the shape of a man wearing jeans and a hooded sweatshirt, bowing down.

John nodded, his own withered hands working slowly on a chunk of clay. "Is that man receiving a blessing or is he bowed in worship? Or could it be that he is being knighted by a king and given a mission?"

"All those things," I said.

John set his own sculpture down. A white horse, beautifully detailed. It was galloping, and its mane crashed on its neck like waves. Flecks of sweat flew from its haunches, and it was clear that the horse was straining, bent forward at the urging of its master. John picked up another chunk of clay and began molding. "Paint," he said, so I picked up some paper and the watercolors. At first nothing came to me, but then an image suddenly carried me away, and as I painted, John spoke.

"Some people stop following Jesus because the world is full of pain." He watched me paint for a minute. "They lose a loved one, or they are harmed by a loved one." He started taking small pieces of clay in various colors and mixing them in his papery hands. "Here they acknowledge a great truth: that God is love. He must be love. And if he is not, then he is no God worth serving.

"But they also make a great mistake, for they assume that the world's pain is his pleasure. This is simply false. Or they will say he cannot know our pain. This, too, is a lie." I could see that in his hands he was fashioning a tiny crown of gold, made to look like thorns. "They will say that he has no power to overcome death—another lie. Love is as strong as death. It burns like a bonfire, like the very flame of the Lord. Water can't put it out. Rivers can't wash it away. Love existed before the first death, and it will remain when death is gone." He rolled out a robe from the clay, shining white in the darkness of the labyrinth.

"We crowded around him at the city gates," John said. "All the people, united by our suffering. We cried out to him, 'Save now, Lord!'" He swiftly wrapped a man-shaped bit of clay into the robe, then set the crown upon its head and the man upon the horse. "We do not follow Jesus because the world is a perfect place." He made a clay sword and put it into the hand of the rider. "We follow him because we desire his Kingdom to come. When he comes, he will make all things right. He will bring justice. And you and I are his humble servants. His representatives. His ambassadors. And we must do our best to bring life and justice, to free the captives, and to bring recovery of sight to the blind. Show me your picture."

I showed him the painting. It was a hand, one of the hands I had felt so vividly on my head, and around it shone a pure light, a seeping of color that bled through the page and into the world. From the center of his hand spilled a slash of red that pooled in the palm and then up and over, running along his fingertips, dripping off the page. "He suffered too," I said.

John reached across and grabbed my hand. "God will live with us. You will speak with him as you did today. We will be his people, and he himself will be with us and be our God. He will wipe every tear from our eyes, and there will be no more death or mourning or crying or pain." Even as he said these words, his voice quavered and a tear ran down his crooked face. "The old order of things will have passed away."

"How can he wipe our tears if there's no more crying?"

John smiled. "Because the tears he will wipe from our eyes will be for the things we've lost in *this* life. After that, there will be no more mourning." He took the sculpture of Christ in his hands. "I have seen all my friends die," he said. "I have seen many grievous things in my life. Here is the lesson I have learned: *Love each other.*"

He took my painting of the hand of Christ and centered it on the table. Above it Christ the King rode his mighty white horse, bringing justice to the world. He took the sculpture I had made of myself and placed it facing Christ, a clear picture of supplication and praise.

"He is our hope." John tapped his finger on the edge of the paper I had painted. "We follow him not only for what he has done in the past—" he touched the sculpture of me on my knees in the labyrinth—"but for what he is doing today." He ran a finger around the mounted Christ. "We follow him because of what he will one day do."

I looked at the white horse, Christ returning to make all things right and do away with death and suffering and mourning once and for all. "I hope he comes quickly," I said.

"Amen." John's eyes reflected my yearning. "Amen."

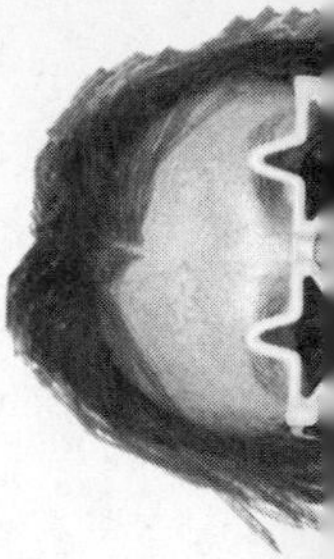

CHAPTER THIRTY-NINE

Function at the Junction

That spring we had a monstrous barbecue at our house. The president of the United States couldn't come, but the sun had shown up, at least. Everyone brought their favorite dishes. My mom brought barbecue, Krista made chicken and dumplings, someone even brought egg foo yong and kidney stew. The house was packed with people, just jammed to the gills with partygoers. The Hate Club—all of them: Sam, Chris, Roland, Alan, Adrian, and Gavin—mixed it up when they weren't arguing with one another about the rise and fall of sequential art. Chris and Joy brought their lovely brood of children, who were running like animals with my kids. Sandy was there, and she had brought her new boyfriend. Shane and the atheists were there, and Sandy introduced them around and made them feel comfortable. My parents and Krista's parents lurked in the crowd, starting conversations, getting to know people. Krista happily produced more food by the moment, and everyone seemed jolly, ecstatic at the first signs of spring and the promise of summer.

I was having the most fun out of everyone there. After

a dramatic conflagration at the grill, I worked on steak, burgers, and salmon for everyone. Grilled vegetables for the vegetarians. Pete was there, moving from group to group, laughing, enjoying himself. Even Daisy seemed content in a corner of the yard, munching on some tender shoots of grass. Jesus was there too. The real Jesus. Not standing around in robes or listening to an iPod or running with his robes hiked up. I couldn't *see* him, but I could sense him taking pleasure in the disparate enjoyments of our friends.

Krista called me and I turned the grill over to my dad. She wasn't in the kitchen, so I ran up the stairs. She was at the top of the stairs, wearing jeans and a green T-shirt, her hair was pulled up onto her head, and she looked marvelous. Stunning. As I came up toward her, she put her arms around me and yanked me close to her. I encircled her with my arms.

"Are you back?" she asked. "You've been distracted for a while."

"I'm back." I pulled her closer and kissed her neck.

"I have something to tell you," she said.

The doorbell rang and I could hear the stampede of children jostling for the front door. Krista pushed me back enough to look me in the eyes. The children roared and clamored from below.

"A DOG!" Zoey called.

"STANDING ON ITS HIND LEGS TO RING THE BELL!" Allie yelled.

I jumped. Only one dog could be so clever. "Houdini Dog!" I said to Krista.

She laughed. "Go! Go get him."

I ran down the stairs and yelled at my dad to guard the meat. I told the guests that Houdini Dog was at the door. They all knew his legend. I burst from the front door, but he was already gone. A crowd of our friends shot from the side gate and ran down the sidewalk to the south, shouting, "This way, Matt, we saw him!"

I ran after them, and we piled around the corner onto the next street. Neighbors came out of their houses to see what all the commotion was, and dogs all over the neighborhood began a chorus of wild barking. Adrian was toward the front of our pack, and he leaped up onto a fence, balancing precariously. "He's crossing through the backyards!"

I decided to catapult over a fence and race through the backyards, but as I propelled myself into the air, I met the fence with my midsection. All the air exploded from my lungs and I fell back onto the sidewalk. I stood shakily, and Roland, Alan, and Gavin lifted me up and threw me over the fence.

"Get out of my yard!" a neighbor yelled, coming out his back door with a shotgun.

"Yes, sir!" I said, and I jumped onto his lawn furniture and over the fence. I could see where Houdini Dog had dug a hole for his escape, so I followed, pushing myself through the hole. A gate swung open and I sped around the corner. I could see the dog's escape route by studying the uncomprehending stares of my neighbors, all turned toward the main road. I was out of breath, but I was determined to catch that dog or, at the very least, to see him.

With a monumental surge of willpower, I ran past the elementary school and came out on Ninety-ninth Street. There he was. A beagle, short but sleek, his coat glossy and his lips pulled back in a dashing canine smile. He barked ecstatically, and as I moved closer, he flipped into the air and landed with a practiced flair in the bed of a speeding truck. His ears flapped in the breeze, as if saying good-bye. His tongue lolled out of his mouth in joyful playfulness. I raised my hand in farewell and he called out with a friendly bark. I watched the truck head west and then turn onto Highway 5. Houdini Dog trundled out of view, but he watched me with those brown eyes until we couldn't see each other any longer.

I ran home, feeling a renewed sense of the immense beauty of the world. My friends had already gone back. I didn't see any of them on the street, and the neighbors had gone indoors again. I was struck by how fortunate I was to live in such a place, to have such friends, to live through another spring. I threw the door open and jumped into the middle of the knot of children, harassing them and tossing them about. I ran up the stairs and grabbed my wife, spinning her around like we were waiting for any excuse to touch one another, like we were dating.

"I saw him," I told her. I danced in place and raised my arms victoriously over my head. She grabbed my arms and put them back around her waist. Then she put her arms around my neck.

"I have something to tell you," she said. She pulled me close and whispered in my ear. As she spoke, it was as if all the joy in my life had been dammed up and the dam had only a few moments ago begun to leak. Now it burst into a million pieces, overwhelmed by the deluge, a riotous explosion of joy. I squeezed her against me. I grabbed her arms and looked at her eyes, where the tears were preparing an expedition across her lovely cheeks.

"Say it again," I said.

She smiled and said, louder, "I'm *pregnant*."

Acknowledgments

A book is not written in a vacuum. This is because one cannot breathe in a vacuum, and space suits are expensive. Since I had to write in the atmosphere, all these people kept influencing me and deserve my thanks. Observe:

This book would not exist in its present form if Wes Yoder (agent and friend) hadn't declined to represent the original sugarcoated collection of Sunday school lessons by saying something along the lines of, "This is no good," and graciously reading the next draft. Many thanks to him and all the fine folks at Ambassador Literary Agency.

I wouldn't have met Wes if not for Gary Thomas, who has been more than generous with his time, insights, and excellent advice.

Sarah "DC" Atkinson, who not only bent over backward but also broke multiple limbs for this book; Jan Long Harris for believing that this book was a good idea; Lisa Jackson, whose insightful comments and feedback took everything good about this book and made it great; Sharon Leavitt for keeping it all running smoothly; Beth Sparkman for the rad cover; George Barna for the great fish and chips and the good advice; Nancy Clausen, Yolanda Sidney, Charlie Swaney, Christy Wong, Adam Sabados, Kevin O'Brien, Caleb Sjogren, and all the rest of the family at Tyndale, who I hope to mention by name in my many future books.

Thanks to my tagline contest winners: Sam Li, Janet Oberholtzer, and Kyle Collins. Thanks also to John Johnson, Dean Christensen, Jim McGuire, and all the Villagers.

Also, special thanks to my guinea pigs, who read various drafts of *Imaginary Jesus* or gave me permission to tell their stories in this book: Chris and Joy Dennis, Shasta Kramer, Dan Weidner, Paula Gamble, Peter Hibbs, everyone with the last name Culbertson (especially Dan, Rachel, Carolyn, and Terry), Joe and Shannon Emery, Adam Huminsky, Jesse Schlender, Ken Cheung, Dave Shackelford, Alexis and Jesse Putnam, Luke Harrison, Keith and Kim Bubalo, Gerry

Breshears, Brian Jannsen, Kerry Little, Sarah Veltkamp, Joe Field, Elders Laurel and Hardy, Sandy Collins, John Rozzelle, Pete Zagorda, Evan Bretzmann, Ryan McReynolds, Herman and Angela Tam, Chris and Susan Zaugg, Selina Tam, Daisy the talking donkey, Amanda Wolf, Andy McCullough, Reid and Tifah Phillips, Dann Stockton, Emily Malloure, Matt Baugher, Sam Stewart, Alan Travis, Roland Belcher, Chris Mendoza, and Gavin Hammon.

To Griffin Gibson for the great author photo. (See more of her work at http://www.griffingibson.com.) Also to Grant Blakeman for his spectacular work on ImaginaryJesus.com. You can contact Grant at http://gb-studio.tv.

My family: Mom, Dad, Lynn, Dave, Dawn, Todd, Kevin, Shimmra, Jonas, Janet, Terry, Ed, Ezra. And especially my beloved daughters: Zoey, Allie, and Myca! I love you guys. Also to all my stinters, past and present (you know who you are), the WSN team, and my BHR minions.

Krista—If you had allowed me to get a monkey as promised, I wouldn't have had time to write this book. Thanks for being my best friend, confidante, wise counselor, and wife. I love you and look forward to many happy years together.

The Lord Jesus Christ is at least partially to blame for my sense of humor, and I sincerely hope he's laughing along with me, or I'm in big trouble. I love you, thanks for everything, and I mean everything.

And, lastly, please write your name here:

____

Continue the conversation with Matt and George from chapter 28!

Visit www.imaginaryjesus.com and www.barna.org for

- ☆ New Barna Group research with surprising (and non-imaginary) statistics about what people *really* think of Jesus
- ☆ A special message from George Barna
- ☆ And much more!

CONTINUE THE *Imaginary Jesus* EXPERIENCE ONLINE

BECOME MATT'S FRIEND!

http://facebook.com/mattmikalatos

Learn the minutia of his day-to-day life!

http://twitter.com/mattmikalatos

READ INTERVIEWS AND SHARE YOUR STORY ABOUT *Imaginary Jesus*.

http://www.imaginaryjesus.com

INVITE MATT TO SPEAK TO YOU.

For information about Matt Mikalatos speaking engagements, please contact:

Ambassador Speakers Bureau
info@AmbassadorSpeakers.com
615.370.4700

Go deeper inside Matt's BIZARRE mind.

Download a free book discussion guide and bonus author notes at http://www.imaginaryjesus.com or www.christianbookguides.com.